TRANSFIXED

WITCHES OF JACKSON SQUARE

A. LONERGAN

Kyla,
you are magic!

Lonergan

TRANSFIXED

To my friends that make each day magical.

CHAPTER ONE

I peered over my shoulder but kept running. Fire exploded next to me and chunks of sheet rock went flying around me.

What the hell?

I didn't slow down even though I was shocked senseless. What was going on? I ducked my head out of instinct and flew down a narrow hallway to my right. My feet slid on the tile but I didn't care. I pushed myself harder trying to get away from the lunatic behind me. Clearly, I was a lunatic too, fireballs?! I must have lost my mind when she had started chasing me. There was no way this was real.

All a dream. Dream. Dream. WAKE UP!

Another fire ball blasted above me. I snickered. This lady had awful aim but then again, I wasn't brave enough to look back and see what she was shooting at me with.

I was about to round another corner when an arm flew out of one of the doors. I let out a very unlady like shriek as I was jerked into the hotel room. I kicked my legs out and my arms, flailing around wildly trying to fight off the woman in front of me. She shook her head and put a finger over her lips. She appeared to be much nicer than the one after me.

"Stupid girl, hush your mouth!" She made a shushing noise before wiggling her fingers at the door.

Did someone slip something in my drink last night?

The night before was foggy, and I had woken up alone in our hotel room. I had stumbled down the hallway to the free breakfast in the lobby only to not make it there when some wild woman started screaming my name, telling me to stop.

I was yanked out of my thoughts when the woman in front of me gripped my arm and pulled me to the window.

I looked at her confused.

"Do you really think she's just going to be okay with not getting through that door? Like she isn't going to try another tactic to get to you?" The woman in front of me rolled her eyes.

I shrugged my shoulders at her, I still didn't trust myself to even think something that wasn't entirely crazy. This was all so crazy, but I had no choice but to follow her. I didn't think she wanted to kill me… yet. It was the better alternative to the woman in the hall, that was for sure. I gulped and followed her.

The woman at the window turned around as she pushed the large panes of glass open. "By the way, I'm Ayre."

I just nodded my head, I wasn't sure if I wanted her to know my name or not. When I got to the window, I stopped. The Mississippi River was high against a small balcony lining the hotel. This wasn't possible. It couldn't be. No company would be stupid enough to build this close to the Mississippi. Not to mention, the hotel I had checked into hadn't been this close to the river. Ayre hopped out to the balcony and held her hand out to help me down. I took it and jumped next to her. I could smell the dirt from the river, and if I leaned over just a tad, I would have been able to touch the murky water. Not that I would, that water was disgusting.

I let my hand trail along the iron railing that separated me from the river.

"What's your name and where is your magi?" Ayre didn't stop walking and wasn't worried about all the windows on the other side of us. It was just a long balcony that resembled a sidewalk connected to the hotel. She seemed comfortable enough with it like this wasn't her first time walking it.

"I'm not sure what you mean," I said, uncertain by what a magi was.

Ayre turned around and gave me a strange look before she pushed open two windows at the end of the walkway. She shook her head before she disappeared inside. I followed her blindly... Like my day could get any worse. Might as well try to make the best of it.

I spun around in a small circle, absolutely stunned. We had ended up in a small shop. By the smells and sounds around me, I knew it was dead center of the French Quarter.

But it couldn't be. The French Quarter wasn't directly off of the Mississippi. I turned to look back through the windows, but they were gone. My eyes searched the walls frantically for the windows we had come through.

Nothing.

I closed my eyes and tried to breathe. There was no way. A soft touch on my shoulder had me jumping through my skin. Ayre gave me a sympathetic look. "Are you all right?"

"We came through windows, right?" I asked, incredulously.

She nodded.

"B-but there are no windows in here." I stammered.

Ayre gave me a smirk before looking down at her hands. Her fingers did a little wiggle, and red sparks danced on the tips. "I'm going to take a gander that you're new to magic."

I swallowed hard, it felt like I had rocks in my throat. "You're right. This is all extremely new, besides what I know from fairytales, of course." My voice sounded squeaky and unsure.

"Forget everything you think you know. But I do have a question." She gave me a concerned look.

"Yes?" I tried to look at anything but her.

"If you're so new to magic, then why do your eyes look like that?"

"Like what?" I didn't want to know. I didn't need to know. I was too afraid.

"Like mine. Like any other magic wielder in this

city." She pointed to her eyes with her delicate fingers.

I got a little closer to Ayre and inspected her eyes. They were bright lavender, quite beautiful. I knew that my eyes looked nothing like hers, mine were as murky as the Mississippi River. I blinked my eyes hard.

"Here," Ayre pushed me toward a souvenir sunglasses rack that had a mirror at the top of it. I didn't let my eyes meet and instead gazed at the spotting of freckles on my nose. "It's nothing to be afraid of, I think they suit you well."

Her words gave me the courage and boost I needed. Sure enough, my eyes were bright lavender too. My hands flew up to my face, and my fingertips brushed the undersides of my eyes gently. They were beautiful and scary. What was happening to me?

"Come on, I'll help you the best I know how." She grabbed my hand and lead me through the back door. The door brought me through to a whole different world. There were jars with eyeballs and fingers in them. Test tubes full of teeth and all sorts of other nasty and odd things. It was everything a tourist would expect to see in The Quarter. In all my years living in Louisiana, I had always dreamed I would have stumbled upon a shop like this. Except I would have hoped it all was fake. I loved the flare of New Orleans and would have believed it to be just that. Flare.

For whatever reason, I knew everything in this small room was very real. A Chinese woman with floor length hair peered at me from behind a table in the corner of the room. There were tarot cards spread out around her and a crystal ball at the far corner of the small structure. Her eyes were a deeper purple than mine and Ayre's. They were almost haunting. The little woman cleared the table then set 4 large boxes on it.

Ayre put her hands on my shoulders and pushed me forward. My legs felt like noodles, and my brain was screaming at me to turn back but I couldn't. I just couldn't move. There was no way this could be a dream, I was never creative enough to come up with something like this. I was from a small town about 70 miles from New Orleans, and I didn't have much family. Wasn't this how the movies went anyway?

Ayre moved toward the counter and looked at the long boxed expectantly.

I let out a laugh. "What are you waiting for Hagrid? Waiting for a wand to choose me?" She gave me a blank stare. "Uh, please don't tell me you haven't seen Harry Potter, and that joke was lost on you."

"Oohh, no I have never seen Harry Potter. We don't like to watch or read stuff like that. Though, a tad bit of it may be true, it gets under our skin more than anything." She rolled her eyes. "Humans always get it wrong."

"Right, of course. Silly me." I muttered under my breath. I approached the counter hesitantly. The Chinese woman looked into my eyes once more before she lifted the lids off of the boxes. Sitting in each of the white boxes were beautiful broaches and pendants of all different shapes and sizes. Shocked was an understatement. I had been expecting wands. "Can I touch them?" I felt like a child for asking.

The woman nodded and sat down, her movements graceful. I let my fingertips trail over the sparkling gems. My fingers stopped on the one that looked to be made out of garnets, the red stones begging for me to pick them up. It was a small circle, no bigger than a quarter. The rocks on it were shaped like little flowers.

When I picked it up, I gasped. Little spikes extended from the underside of it and grew. They almost looked like spider legs. Much to my surprise, they almost were. The short legs stopped growing, and it jumped from my fingers onto the top of my other hand. It walked until it was at my wrist. It dropped onto my skin there, and the legs began to grow until they wrapped all the way around my arm. I felt my mouth drop open. That wasn't normal.

The little legs started to sprout little legs until they all connected and looked like lace around my arm. The little broach almost resembled a watch now. I wiggled my arm around testing the flexibly of it. It moved like it was a second skin.

"What is this?" I moved my arm again watching the thing curiously.

"It's like a wand but more discreet. It will help you wield magic easier." Ayre gave me a little smile and held her hand up. On her middle finger was a small ring. The center of it was knots of gems. I would have never guessed it. "Mine shrunk to fit me. I like little spells with my fingers, and this gem sensed that. They know where to go and how to adapt to you."

"So is this a magi?"

She nodded then turned to leave through the door we had come through.

"Wait!" Ayre turned back at the desperate squeak that had escaped me. "Don't we need to pay her?"

She let out a small laugh. It even sounded magical. "No, there is a magi for every witch in the city. I knew that if you were really one of us, a magi would do what it did. If you weren't, well, it probably wouldn't have gone too well."

"What would have happened?" I asked, scared of the answer.

She narrowed her eyes at me. "I don't even know your name, you're lucky you got a magi."

I felt myself blush. "I'm sorry, I guess you have trusted me a bit, and I haven't given you much to go off of. I'm Freya." I offered her a small smile.

"Glad to finally know your name." She continued through to leave the little shop, but something caught my eye and made me stop.

A small shining ball sat on the shelf above the door. It was a deep red like the stones on my Magi. I tried to get a closer look, but it was too high. Ayre had already disappeared through the door, but I didn't mind. I could catch up. This, for some reason, seemed important. I peered at the shelves around the door looking for a way to get up to it.

Ayre popped her head through the doorway

and gave me an odd look before peering above her at the small sphere. She scoffed. "Those are apparently dragon eggs."

"Apparently?" I raised my eyebrows.

"There's no such thing as dragons," she muttered, right before she disappeared again. I didn't care what she said, I still couldn't shake the thought that it was important, whatever it was.

"For you." I jumped out of my skin again at the sound of the Chinese woman behind me. I couldn't take much more of this.

She was holding a step stool and a backpack. The backpack was made out of dark leather and had a small pocket on the front of it. She climbed up the step stool and brought the little 'dragon egg' down with her. She slipped it into the front pocket then gave me the backpack. Her eyes were practically glowing as she said, "Keep it safe."

A chill ran through my body, and I wondered about the egg before I shouldered the backpack and followed Ayre. She was waiting for me on the other side of the doorway with a bored expression on her face.

She gave the pack a curious glance before rolling her eyes and leading the way out of the small tourist shop. The humidity was like a smack to the face as we walked out onto the street. Jazz was playing softly somewhere nearby, and I could faintly smell pee behind the smell of beignets. I crinkled my nose in disgust and tried to ignore it. New Orleans wasn't the cleanest city, but the sweet pastries made up for it.

"So, how did we get here from the hotel?" I raised an eyebrow at Ayre.

She ignored my question. "Why are you in New Orleans?" She flicked her long kinky hair over her shoulder and kept walking.

"I just graduated. It was a celebration, we finally have some freedom. Well, at least I do." I shrugged, not sure of why I was giving her so much information.

Ayre stopped and let me catch up to her. "You probably need to let your fellow students know you won't be meeting up with them later."

It was my turn to stop. "And why not?"

"You don't belong in their world anymore, Freya." She turned to me and frowned.

I didn't know why her words didn't bother me. I had always figured I hadn't belonged. I had never felt like part of the family with my foster group. I had never fit in, I had always been different.

"Would you like to go back to the hotel to collect your things?" She asked with sympathy.

I thought of the sheetrock exploding around me and knew I wouldn't be going back to get my few clothes and my phone charger. I shook my head at her. "No, there's nothing left for me there."

Ayre looked surprised at my words. "Okay, so is there anything you do want to get?"

I scratched my head and tried to remember where I had parked my car the night before. It was still a little hazy, and I had only had a few drinks. Granted, I had never had alcohol before. "My car but I can't seem to remember where I parked it last night. It's a little foggy."

A concerned look passed over Ayre's face. "Did you drink alcohol?"

I nodded my head.

"Alcohol affects us differently than humans. It doesn't mix well with the magic in our blood and gives us odd reactions. We'll worry about your car later." She grabbed my hand and yanked me forward.

I accepted her words and hoped the memories came back to me soon. I didn't like being out of control, I didn't like not knowing what was happening. It was all just too much.

I was trying to sort through my erratic thoughts when Ayre stopped and pulled me into an alley.

Odd.

She looked around us before approaching a door at the end of the alley, it was dark and the stench of pee was strong, there was another smell that I couldn't detect, that was just as awful. I watched as Ayre pressed her Magi into the keyhole beneath the doorknob. The sizeable french door groaned before swinging open. Ayre grabbed my hand and pulled me through the opening before the door swung closed behind us. It hit the door frame so hard that dust exploded around us like confetti. I tried to dodge it, but there was no use. I cringed before I had the chance to look around me.

My mouth dropped open at the sight before me. I couldn't believe what I was seeing. We were in a vast courtyard that had a massive garden surrounding it, then behind the garden was balconies and iron railings that lead to French doors and a second story, which was just as breathtaking. The stucco was starting to peel and crack, with vines sprouting out from them.

Arye looked at me expectantly. "Eh, eh!" She gave me a goofy grin before continuing. "Welcome to the Master's Compound. There are a few empty rooms, which is pretty common with all the students leaving for the summer."

"A few? This whole place looks empty!" My voice was a hushed whisper. I was still in awe.

"Well, of course, witches have day jobs too!" She had a point. It was the middle of the day.

I followed the woman up the iron steps to the second story and trailed behind her, as she pushed through the pale distressed doors. I took in my surroundings once more in adoration. It was truly magnificent.

There was a considerable mahogany rice bed against the brick accent wall. The massive bed was turned down with a lilac duvet and matching throw pillows. Beside the bed was a matching step stool.

A miniature writing desk took up space in front of the lace curtains covering the windows. The windows stretched from floor to ceiling and over-looked the garden below. Across the room was a dresser that had a spacious mirror hanging over it. I rubbed my eyes. I had never been in such a magnificent room before.

"Wow," I swallowed hard and tried to make sense of everything happening to me.

"This can be your room, that is, if you like it." Ayre winked at me. "It's pretty great, isn't it?"

I nodded unable to form words for just how amazing this all was. It had to be a dream. Then it occurred to me that there was still a woman out there, searching for me. A woman that had known my name and was trying to harm me. "What about the woman that was coming after me?"

Ayre gave me a frown. "I don't know who she was. I'm waiting for Camey Master's to get home and we'll figure it out then. I wish I had more answers for you." She touched my shoulder affectionately. "We will go get your things tomorrow. Go ahead and rest. I'm sure you're physically and emotionally exhausted after all the things that have happened today."

Ayre disappeared through the doors, and I didn't mind. She was right, my mind was reeling, and I wasn't sure where to make sense of any of it. The curtains on the doors blew around in the breeze, and for once, I didn't mind the heat in the end of May. Another day, I would have slammed the doors closed and blasted the A/C. I was not one for the humidity but today didn't seem to be too bad.

I took a deep breath. What was I doing here? I had blindly followed Ayre through all of this and hadn't stopped to really think. I set my backpack on the small dresser and gasped at my reflection in the mirror. I was indeed glad that the compound had been empty, that was for sure.

My strawberry blonde hair was ruffled around my head, and my new lavender eyes were wide in shock. I narrowed my eyes at my reflection, and for once in my life, I hoped my brown eyes would come back. My pale skin looked slightly flushed, but that wasn't unusual with the Louisiana heat and humidity. I made my way to the large bed and pulled myself onto it.

What now?

I rested my chin on my palm and closed my eyes. I knew without a shadow of a doubt that the next few hours would be a waiting game.

CHAPTER TWO

I had realized that I had dozed off until a strange noise in the room had me sitting up straight in the bed. I rubbed my sleep filled eyes with my fist and tried to get them to adjust to the darkness. Something unfamiliar itched on my wrist, and just as I was about to scratch at it, the rustling in the corner of the room got louder. Then a giggle sounded. I rubbed my eyes again.

There were two people in the corner of the room, and they looked to be struggling, but I knew better. I heard another giggle and almost gagged. "I love the term 'get a room' but not when it is mine." My voice was unwavering and stronger than usual. I didn't typically dare to stand up for myself.

That's new.

"What the hell?" A deep voice timbered through the room. If he hadn't been tangled up with someone else, I would have thought it to be attractive.

The body that belonged to the masculine voice waved his arm over his head, and the entire room was lit in a soft glow. The man stood up to his full height, and my eyes got wide. He was easily the most attractive man I had ever seen. He was wearing a dark navy suit; the bottom of his white shirt had come untucked during his tussle with the girl standing behind him. She was hastily trying to fix her short dress and the sleeves that had somehow come off of her arms.

The man was oddly staring at me, so I patted down my hair self consciously. I tended to be a wild sleeper.

"Ohhhh, Sterling! Her eyes are the same color as yours! Is she the sister you mentioned?" The woman screeched.

"No!" His voice boomed around the room, a little too loud!

The girl looked confused. She pulled on her blonde ponytail and cocked her head at me like an animal in thought. "Then why is she in your room?"

"That's a great question!" Sterling folded his arms over his chest and hiked his eyebrows up. I couldn't tear my eyes away from his bulging muscles pressed against the sleeves of his suit. I didn't understand how that could be comfortable, but I guessed it probably wasn't for comfort.

"Ayre told me that I could stay in here." I folded my arms over my chest in defiance.

"Ayre! Ayre! Of course! Ha." He turned away from me and focused his eyes on the short girl beside him. "We will continue this later. I'll call you." He brushed a white strand of hair away from her face before turning back to me. "You can't stay here, I hope you know that."

I shrugged my shoulders. I was used to power struggled in my past foster homes. I pushed myself from the glorious bed and grabbed my new backpack before exiting the room.

"That's it?" Sterling called from behind me. I was too new here to try to start a turf war. That wasn't my style. I was the kind of girl that kept her head down and didn't interfere. I didn't bother replying. I probably didn't belong here, to begin with. It was a never-ending cycle of being no one.

The courtyard was the only other area that I had been to, I found a wooden swing across the way and took residence there. It was comfortable and had a beautiful view of the star. They were about the only constant thing in my life.

"Oh my gosh, Sariah! Sariah!" A woman screamed from across the courtyard. "You're back!"

The name was repeated several times more before I finally looked up to find the woman right in front of me staring. "Sariah?" Her voice dropped.

I frowned, confused. "I'm sorry, I think you have me confused with someone else."

Tears were streaming down her tan face. She was beautiful and reminded me of Ayre. She had long brown wavy hair that hit her mind back. She was very curvy in all the right places even though she was much taller than me. "You look so much like her, it's uncanny." She wiped her eyes with the back of her hand and gave me a hesitant look. "Sariah was my best friend, and I haven't seen her in a very long time."

"I'm very sorry to hear that." I pulled my bag closer to me and tried to get comfortable.

"Where are my manners? I'm Camey Master. I'm the high priestess of this coven. Are you passing through town and needing a place to stay?" Where her voice of hope had been, it was now replaced with a professional business quality that had probably taken her long time to perfect.

"I'm new to all of this, actually. I don't really know where I belong. I'm Freya." I looked at my lap before I saw a flash of concern cross Camey's face. "What do you mean?" She found a spot beside me.

"I'm not entirely sure what I mean. Ayre saved my life. Apparently, I have magic and magic exists, and I don't know what else is happening to me besides the rude guy that kicked me out of the room upstairs that Ayre gave me." The words tumbled from my mouth at a speed I didn't know I possessed.

"Ayre!" Camey's voice cracked with power as it shook the compound. I shrunk back into the bench and tried to disappear.

"Yes, mom?" Ayre sounded bored as she rounded the corner. When she noticed me, she narrowed her eyes. "A magi chose her. I would have never brought her here if she hadn't had one. I don't know who is after her, but she needed a safe place and people that she can trust to teach her her god given gifts. Dark magic was being used, and we don't need her falling into their hands now do we."

"Why didn't you call me, Ayre?" Camey's voice

had lost the fire it had had before and was softer now.

"There was so much going on, and I knew that Freya needed rest. It's a lot for someone to take in, I would imagine. I figured tomorrow would be a better day to introduce her to the coven and her new life." Ayre shrugged, nonchalantly.

Ayre took a seat on the other side of me and draped her arm over the back of the swing. Then she crinkled her nose and looked at me. "Speaking of rest, why aren't you sleeping?"

I could feel the heat taking over my face. I had already divulged that information to her mother, and now I felt even more embarrassing tattling again. "Uh,"

"You put her in my bed." I startled hard at Sterling speaking from the shadows.

I wasn't the only one startled. Camey had her hand at her throat. "Sterling! Manners, son!"

My mind was spinning. It almost made sense, but it didn't. Why would Ayre have put me in Sterling's room? Certainly, she knew where her brother slept. That was when I saw the resemblance between them. Sterling was tall like his mother and had darker skin like them. His hair was buzzed short, but I could just barely see that the color resembled both of theirs as well.

"Would you like to explain why you put her in your brother's room?" Camey folded her arms over her chest and stood up from the swing.

"I figured it would be nice to shake things up a bit. I certainly didn't think he would bring a girl home and that's how this would all play out." Ayre winked at her brother before leaving her spot next to me. She didn't turn back as Sterling let out a menacing growl.

"You pranked her last week, remember? You know you deserve it, but our new guest does not. We need to be gracious hosts. I know you don't want to have another lecture about your female friends." Camey looked to me with sympathy. "You can have Sterling's room until further notice. Its better suited for you anyhow. Purple isn't your color, Sterling."

He scowled at his mother. "I don't do much sleeping there anyway." He winked at his mother as she walked away.

"You're lucky to have her." My voice came out in a whisper.

"Excuse me? What is that supposed to mean?" His eyes shot daggers at me.

"I would do anything to have a mother. Belonging would be nice for once." He had the audacity to roll his eyes at me. "I'm not sure what your problem is, you said it yourself, you don't do much sleeping there anyway, I doubt it'll be a permeant arrangement. In fact, I can't wait to get as far away from you as possible."

It wasn't my fault all of this was happening to me. I didn't deserve such a hateful person to come and muck it up even further. He tried to say something more, and I held my hand up. I didn't have any interest in continuing the conversation. I bit my tongue as I walked back to Sterling's room, trying to hold back tears. I wasn't usually the sensitive one. Foster care had hardened me and prepared me for the real world, or so I had thought. Things like this didn't typically get under my skin. I had had my fair share of bullies and abuse in the system, but there was just something about Sterling that got under my skin.

CHAPTER THREE

STERLING

The nerve of that woman. She had been the one that had ruined my night. How dare she act that way toward me! I walked up the steps behind her. Her back was ramrod straight, and her head was held high. There was a part of me that felt guilty for being such a jerk to her, but the other part of me was too sexually frustrated to get out of my angry haze.

I took the room right next to mine and winked at her as she looked back at me before closing the door behind her. I had been shocked to find her in my bed. I had been so upset that she had interrupted my fun that I hadn't realized I had an equally hot, if not more, woman in my bed. That was the only thing I regretted, a mad woman wasn't going to jump in bed with you, and I had done it all wrong. Since when had my game gotten this bad?

I closed the doors behind and laid on the daybed pushed against the wall. I knew my bed was pushed against the same wall. Growing up we had many students in and out of the compound, I had learned really early how thin the walls were and where everything was located. Behind my clothes in the closet was a trap door, barely big enough to crawl through that led to this room. I had had my fair share of sneaking in and out of here to see girls and to defy my parents. I had given more scares than anything.

I stripped my suit coat off and threw it to the floor. There was no use in keeping it, there was a nice tear in the sleeve now from it being too small. I knew I should have gone up a size. I unbuttoned my white shirt and tossed it on top. I pushed the en-suite bathroom door open and grabbed a towel.

MY SHOWER WAS SHORT, I was still angry, and the cold water was only making my nerves worse. I hadn't thought of the fact that the new girl would need a shower too. Then I remembered that all my clothes were still in my room also and it made me even madder. That was when I remembered the hidden door again and listened to make sure she was settled in my bed first before I turned creeper. With my sisters pranking and the new girl next door, there was no way I was sleeping naked or in dirty clothes.

I pressed my ear against the wall and listened to her get comfortable in bed before there was silence. I decided it was my time to make my move. I crawled through the cubby hole, almost losing my towel in the process and tiptoed to the closet door. The only thing I needed from my actual room was my boxers, and I knew I could have gone without them, but curiosity drove me to open the door and gaze at the woman lying in my bed. The moon was shining through the lace curtains onto her bareback.

I gulped and tried not to think of her rolling over in her sleep. I kept my eyes on her as I made my way across the room to my dresser. I quickly got my pair of boxers out and tiptoed back across the room. Her fiery hair was spread out on the pillow around her like a halo. I hadn't noticed her freckles before, but it made sense with her soft red hair. I closed the closet behind me and snagged a pair of pajama pants and a white t-shirt.

CHAPTER FOUR

FREYA

I made Sterling's bed quickly. Not wanting to give him any more reasons to hate me. I then started to pace in front of the bed. I was wearing a pair of basketball shorts that I had found in the top drawer of the dresser and a white T-shirt from the closet. I felt terrible. This would definitely give Sterling fuel for his hatred fire. I paced and paced some more until finally there was a knock on the door. I hadn't slept well at all and had been awake for hours staring at the worn wooden boards of the ceiling. I had dreamt that Sterling had come into the room and watched me sleep with hatred.

I was obviously being ridiculous, but the man unnerved me and possibly even frightened me,

What guy that handsome wouldn't be scary anyway?

Ayre pushed the doors open and immediately started laughing. "Oh, oh, this is great. Sterling is really going to hate me now."

"Hate you? He's going to hate me more!" I threw my hands into the air.

"He doesn't hate you. He's just a jerk." Ayre shrugged her shoulders like it couldn't be helped.

"I thought it was both." I frowned.

"Nope, if he hated you he would have never let you sleep in his bed. I don't care if our mother is the High Priestess, he would have raised hell. Literally." She then grabbed my hand and yanked me out of the room. "But we need to hurry, he can't see you-"

"Wow! Don't those articles of clothing look familiar." Sterling's voice boomed behind us. I flinched, and of course, Ayre grinned. There was nothing like sibling rivalry, I imagined.

I started to apologize before Ayre interrupted me. "You don't expect her to walk around here nude, do you?"

I was frozen and afraid to turn around then Sterling said something that made it impossible for me to face him. "That wouldn't be so bad." Heat traveled up my neck and into my face.

I watched out of the corner of my eye as Ayre rolled hers. "Don't be a cad. I'll be sure to put her into some of my clothes then I'll take her shopping."

Shopping? Most of my clothes were in my car. I only needed my car.

"You would have to run that by me first, and you have not." I finally turned around to see Sterling leaning against the iron railing wearing plaid pajama pants and a white T-shirt.

Ayre gave him a bored look. "That's the coven's money. You forget that I have my own."

Sterling gave her an annoyed look before retreating into his bedroom. I was almost worried about my backpack until I remembered that he practically hated me... why would he be interested in touching my things?

"WHERE DID you last see your car?" Ayre waved me through a big oak door on the first story that led to a room fit for royalty.

"Woah, this is even better than Sterlings room."

I spun around. The bed pushed against the brick wall was even more significant than the one upstairs, and there was cream pinstripe wallpaper on the rest of the walls. A gold duvet covered the messy bed and pillows were littered everywhere. She then pulled me into a humongous walk-in closet. The shoes had their own wall.

She giggled at my expression. "Isn't it grand? My mother has the best taste. I get my style from her. You could actually go shopping in both of our closets and not put a dent in them. We have too much, but sometimes there is that need." She ran her hands down the length of some dresses. "Ya know?"

I shook my head. "No, I don't know. I've never really had anything nice. I owned mostly hand me downs from my friends that felt bad for me."

Ayre's face fell. "Are you serious?"

I nodded my head and ducked out of the closet, if she wanted me to wear something, she would have to pick it out. I was starting to feel over-whelmed again.

"Do you want to talk about it?" Ayre laid some dresses down beside me, and that was when I realized she was wearing a dress too, but her dress was lavender, and it matched her eyes. The ruffle sleeves barely covered her shoulders, and the hem touched her knees. Her sandals were modest and a simple nude.

"Talk about what?" I fingered the lace on pastel green dress and knew that I would never be able to afford such a thing.

"What you went through. Your childhood." She bit the inside of her lip causing it to pucker in.

"There is nothing to talk about. I was poor, that's about it. Nothing special." I shrugged it off, I really didn't want to talk about my past.

"What about your parents?" She picked up all the other dresses but the green one and put them away.

When she came back, I gave her a severe look. "I don't know who my parents are. I've been in foster care for as long as I can remember."

She probably sensed my discomfort and stopped talking. She held up the dress and took it off its hanger. She pushed me into the closet to change.

The dress was beautiful on me. It complimented my porcelain skin tone and my soft reddish-blonde hair. It was always different. It either looked strawberry blonde or fiery red. It changed on a whim, I had always chalked it up to be my imagination. I looked down at my magi, and things started to make more sense. When I pushed the closet door open, I came face to face with Sterling. I made sure my face was blank of all emotion.

I didn't need his judgment ass in my life. He was taking his clothes from Ayre with a nasty look on his face but when he turned to me... it changed. He looked surprised.

"Yeah, I know, I clean up nice." I didn't give him the opportunity to reply and instantly started talking to Ayre. "I'm supposed to be meeting the coven today?"

She smacked her palm to her forehead. "I completely forgot and should have gotten you up earlier. Everyone has left for the day, but that means that we have time to get breakfast and really search for your car!"

She jumped up and down like it was the best thing in the world to have to go out into the Louisiana heat.

Sterling face had so much lack of interest when he spoke. "She'll do anything to get out of the compound. This is going to be the best day ever!" He rolled his eyes before making his exit.

CHAPTER FIVE

STERLING

She was different.

I could see it in the way she held herself and the way she spoke, but I couldn't put my finger on it. She didn't act like all the witches around here. I knew she was new to all of this, but even the humans around New Orleans worked a certain way. There was something there, and I would be damned if I didn't try to figure it out.

By the time they had made it back, I had already gone through her empty leather sack. I had found the dragon egg, though I wasn't sure why my sister had let her get it with her magi. The witches on bourbon rubbed me the wrong way with their dumb creatures, especially the 'dragon eggs' they sold there. There were many things that existed, but dragons weren't one of them.

I heard the massive iron doors slam closed, and I didn't bother with covering my tracks. I tossed Freya's leather sack onto the bed and took my time exiting my bedroom. The new girl and my sister were carrying a few bags, and I wondered if shopping had been in the cards. Since the backs were cheap and falling apart, I doubted that they had. I could hear the new girl's voice echoing around the courtyard.

"I didn't realize we were in Jackson Square. How is this even possible?" I rolled my eyes at her even though she couldn't see me. Couldn't she put the pieces together already? Magic.

Ayre giggled at her nativity, but I couldn't hear what she said back. When they made it up the steps, and I could see them making their way toward me, I leaned casually in the doorway.

"Have a fun time?" I crossed my arms over my chest.

Newbie ignored me, and Ayre beamed. "Oh yes! You should see her little car, it is very quaint."

"Didn't have a good time, Newbie?" She whipped around so fast, I thought her hair was going to kill me.

"For one, asshole, I have a name, and if you don't want a permeant nickname too, then I suggest you learn it, its Freya. Two, don't speak to me ever." She gave me such a harsh glare that I didn't say anything. There was no need for a response. She passed me up in the doorway and put her shoulder in my ribs, and it actually hurt.

"You can't stay in here again. I need my stuff, and I'm not about to do what I did last night again." I could have slapped myself. Dammit.

"Excuse me?" She whipped around again. Her eyes got big. "You came in here last night while I slept." Her face got red as she looked down at her chest in horror.

"I didn't see anything, you were sleeping your stomach. Don't freak out." I rolled my eyes. Women were so dramatic.

"My real question is, how did you get in? I locked the doors!" Her eyes searched me for a magi, and when she didn't find one, they narrowed.

Ayre smirked and marched past us both. She pushed the closet open and swept her hand forward. "I should have known he would stoop this low. He did this when he was a kid." She parted my clothes and revealed the door there.

What happened next, I would have never

predicted. Freya pulled her hand back and where I was preparing myself for a slap. She let her fist fly. I heard a crunch as it connected with my nose. My vision swam for a second as I touched the tender cartilage.

"Next time you feel the need to peep on me, I'll damage something much more valuable." She kicked her foot up just a few inches from my crotch. I stepped away from my room in horror. I had never met such a feisty woman, besides my sister. But then again, she was a redhead.

CHAPTER SIX

FREYA

I took a deep breath and tried to calm my erratic heart rate. I had never felt so furious! I picked the pillow up from the bed and let out a shriek into its feathery contents. By the time I was done, I didn't feel any better, in fact, I felt worse and now had a headache. I pushed my hair from my face and worked hard to calm my nerves, again.

I had never had a temper like this before. I had never felt like I couldn't control myself before. I had usually been level-headed my entire life. I was the calm one in the group homes that kept everyone together and sane. This wasn't like me. I clenched my fists in front of me and started to shake.

What was happening to me?

I let out a scream as lightning burst from my

fingers. The drapes across the room caught on fire, and that was enough to cool me down. I ran to the curtains and stomped on them, putting the small flames out.

Sparks tingled on my fingertips and rage lit up in my heart once again. I couldn't control it. A knock at the door simmered me down. I tucked my electric hands into the pockets on my dress and plastered a smile on my face. If there was something that I was good at; it was putting a fake smile on my face. I had had enough practice throughout the years.

Ayre pushed the door open and gave me a curious glance before looking at my feet. Shoot! I had forgotten about the burnt fabric there. I kicked it away from me, all while smiling suspiciously.

"You can't hide the fact that you just used magic in here. It stinks of rage and burnt fabric." She cocked an eyebrow at me.

"I'm not sure what you are talking about." I continued to push the fabric with my foot. I couldn't stop incriminating myself, apparently. Ugh.

" Magic leaves behind a particular smell. It is coating the room. And if that didn't give it away, the burnt curtains certainly did." Ayre crossed her arms over her chest.

" I don't know what's going on with me. I couldn't control it." Then I realized I was still wearing the magi. I wrapped my fingers around it and tried to pry it off. It wasn't budging. It was almost as if it was embedded into my skin, connected down to the bone.

"I wouldn't try that if I were you." Ayre shook her head and leaned against the wall, observing me.

"Why not?" I asked, getting angry once again.

"Your magi is apart of you now. You can't just take it off. Your magic calls to it and holds it in place. I've never heard of someone being able to remove theirs, and the stories that I have heard weren't good ones."

"What's the worst thing that could happen?" I shrugged my shoulders, trying to fake that I wasn't afraid of ripping the thing from my arm even though I was terrified.

"It could rip your magic from your soul." She frowned at me. "Ya know, no big deal, at all." She rolled her eyes at me.

That did frighten me and before I could reply she grabbed my hand and pulled me from my thoughts and the room. "Emotions fuel our magic. I wish I could tell you that it would get easier but unfortunately, it won't." She led me out of the courtyard and straight into a festival.

This was the New Orleans I loved. The families and all the vendors in the streets. The smell of coffee and beignets floated around me.

An older gentleman with chocolate colored skin played saxophone on the street corner while people crowded around him. He leaned forward then back, completely lost in his own music. When we had left the compound earlier that morning, the streets had been empty and Barron. Now they were full of life and love. People of all shapes and nationalities took pictures and spoke excitedly in different languages,

The sun was hidden behind gray clouds and offered relief from the usual Southern heat. Cafe Du Monde was bustling like usual in front of us and my mouth watered at the thought of their pastries. Ayre motioned me forward and grabbed a table quickly. Usually, the line was down the street, but this morning, there were few people waiting. Ayre winked at me and wiggled her fingers. The people that had been standing in line looked up confused and left altogether. Ayre got up and got our order placed, and within minutes she had a mountain of powdery pastry goodness sitting in front of me.

"Food always helps me feel better." I couldn't have agreed more.

I carefully picked up a beignet and tried to not spill the sugar everywhere. Just as I was about to take a generous bite, Sterling slipped into the seat across from me and gave me a cocky grin. I inhaled suddenly, and the sugary goodness shot up my nose and all over my face. I placed the beignet down hastily all while coughing uncontrollably. Sterling rolled his eyes and Ayre waved her hand in front of my nose. "Avai!"

My coughing stopped and my nose cleared. Ayre gave Sterling a death glare. "Perfect timing…"

Speaking of perfect timing. My nose started to run, and I hastily whipped at it until I noticed the color on my fingers.

Red.

I watched in horror as it dripped into the mountain of white sugar. Sterling scowled, and Ayre gave me a frightened glance. I grabbed a handful of napkins and tried to soak up the blood coming from my nose.

"That's nasty, what's wrong with you?" Sterling snorted.

I shook my head. I didn't know what was happening to me. The more I focused on it, the more blood flowed. I needed to concentrate on anything but my ailment.

"Something isn't right." Ayre waved her hand in front of my face and muttered incantations. Nothing worked. "This is magic-induced. I can't stop it."

Sterling's face went serious then as he looked around us. The streets had cleared, and the music had stopped. Which was very unlike New Orleans. After a few minutes of us looking around, the sky grew dark as the clouds covered the sun. Laughing started in the distance and echoed off of all the buildings around us.

"Do you think you could escape us just by befriending some little witches?" At the woman's voice, I watched as Sterlings fingers lit up in an orange flame. I stood there transfixed. Then almost as if it were on cue, Ayre's fingers did the same, but instead of fire or lightning like mine, hers was a rainbow of different colors, jumping between her hands. It looked like small bolts of energy surging around her body.

Sterling looked at my shocked face and smirked. "She's the high priestesses daughter, her magic is ancient and powerful."

"But you are her son?" I stayed alert, turning about, looking for the woman coming for me.

"It's not the same." He winked before he went flying backward close to the statue of General Jackson.

"Little girl, we have searched high and low, and here you finally are!" The woman came into view than with her hands raised high above her head. She was the woman that had chased me throughout the hotel. Her hair flew around her head in a halo, and the wind picked up around us. Ayre shoved her hands to her sides, and her eyes lit up. She was ready to take on anything.

Me? Not so much.

I tapped on my magi, hoping that it would kick start something. Where was the magic when I actually needed it? My magi had wasted precious magic and energy on the stupid drapes instead of saving up for this psycho.

"Your mother has been waiting for you to come back to New Orleans. It's been years, and finally, your magic is developed enough for us to sense you." Speaking of psycho...

Ayre gave me a confused look. I shrugged my shoulders. "I don't have a mom. Never have."

"Sariah will be pleased to have you back. She's

been needing your magic for some time." There they were with that name again. The woman took a few steps forward, and I took a few back. Out of the corner of my eye, I watched Sterling creeping along the side of a building.

"I don't know who Sariah is! I don't have a mom, and I'm tired of all these new things happening in my life!" Anger built up inside of me and one minute the crazy lady was smiling at me like a lunatic and the next a lightning bolt dropped from the sky and burnt her to ashes. Sterling fell back in shock, just a few feet away from the result of my anger. He scrambled backward and gave me a look of horror.

Ayre's eyes were wide. I wiped at my still bleeding nose and rubbed my magi affectionately. I wasn't sure what had happened, but I could dig it. Sterling approached us slowly then shook his head and turned away.

"That was incredible," Ayre said as she took my hand.

"Thank you," I replied, shocked and self-conscious.

It has been a very long time since I have seen power like that." Ayre circled me slowly. "Are you sure you've never used magic before?"

"What a dumb question," Sterling said as sat down in one of the iron chairs by Cafe Du Monde. "Like she could use magic without a magi. Her magic would rip through her and kill her. The magis are here for a reason. Don't ever forget that."

I looked down at my hands to find sparks jumping between my fingers. I closed my hands into fists and pressed them to my sides. Sterling was looking at me with newfound curiosity, and I didn't blame him. I had enough interest for all of New Orleans.

Ayre gave me another handful of napkins and looked around the empty street. "We should probably get going."

There were no complaints from me. An empty New Orleans was creepy enough, even in broad daylight.

CHAPTER SEVEN

STERLING

Her nose wouldn't stop bleeding. No matter what we did or tried, it just wouldn't stop. When we made it back to the compound, my mother rushed to her side. Her eyes got huge, and I knew she was on the verge of a freakout.

"You're being tracked." She said under her breath. "That's why the bleeding won't stop." She looked to me with confusion. "What happened out there? You were supposed to be keeping watch!"

I scratched my forehead and shrugged. "How am I supposed to do that? The girl is a walking magnet for trouble. She hasn't been a witch for more than a week, and she already has enemies!"

My mother looked around in wild panic. I

wondered how she had ever gotten the title of High Priestess. She couldn't handle anything that gave her a lot of stress.

Where was my father when I needed him?

I pinched the bridge of my nose in frustration. I was supposed to be enjoying my summer, not babysitting my sister's dumb friend. I seemed to have the best luck lately.

Not.

I pulled my magi from my breast pocket and checked the time. I was about to miss the music festival because my mom was erratic and couldn't keep it together in a crisis and some new girl was dumped onto our front porch. I took a deep breath and focused my energy, well, I damn well desperately tried to. It was getting harder and harder to do so with my mother freaking out.

I put my hand on my chest, right above my magi and whispered, "levaí," Orange energy pulsed and danced around my body. My magic moved and reacted differently than everyone else's in the coven. My mother stopped her clucking and finally started to calm down. Exactly what I had intended to happen with my magic. I was the only one that could get through her craze haze.

"I have places to be, please tell me that you can

handle this till dad gets back." I was getting more irritated as the seconds passed.

She glared at me. "Yes, I'm the High Priestess, not him. I am perfectly capable of handling all of this on my own."

"Of course you are," I said under my breath as I walked away. If she thought she could do anything then who was I to stop her? When I made it back to my sleeping quarters, I stripped down to my boxers and pulled on some old clothes. Khaki shorts and a white t-shirt, you didn't wear anything nice to a paint festival.

For whatever reason, my magi had never been attached to my skin. I pulled it from my breast pocket on my suit, and it immediately formed into a long chain and the pocket watch shrunk to about the size of a quarter. A pocket watch magi were practically unheard of these days, but I loved the classic feel to it, and it helped pull my suits together. The magic in it just knew what to do. The only downside was, I couldn't use magic without it. I had forgotten it once as a child, and the unfathomable migraine that had followed had made sure that I wouldn't forget it again and I hadn't. I had also been one of the youngest to receive their magi. Most witches didn't receive theirs until the age of 8.

Mine called to me when I was just turning 4. My parents had made sure that I always wore something dapper after that, making sure that I kept the role up with my pocket watch.

The style had eventually grown on me and I hardly ever changed, unless… A female friend invited me to a rave. I couldn't say no to those, and it seemed as if my magi agreed. I stretched my arms above my head and felt the magic course through my veins. There was honestly nothing like it. I cracked my neck and slipped on some old vans.

When I opened the French doors to the compound, there was mass chaos as my mother didn't know what the hell to do. I didn't plan on doing anything until several other witches gave me a look. I pinched the bridge of my nose again and pulled my phone from my pocket.

"Housekeeping?" A massive French accent floated through the phone.

"Real funny, dad." I rolled my eyes. My dad had a dry humor like no one else.

"What's up, buddy?" I winced at his nickname for me, I had never been a fan of it.

"Mom is having her typical freakout." I sighed. "We have a new girl that is causing a little havoc."

His deep chuckle was a breath of fresh air. "So I

have heard," He let out a louder laugh. "I also heard how you two met and I must say, you have the best timing."

I desperately wanted to laugh along with him, but there was no way I could. I still didn't find the redhead amusing. What my dad said next had me wishing I hadn't called at all.

"I've also heard she is quite a looker."

"How about we not head that direction and go back to mom?" I pulled the phone away from my face, contemplating whether or not I should hang up.

"That would be fantastic, except there is nothing I can do for you or her. I will be stuck at the office for at least another hour. No emergency can pull me from this case, I'm sorry."

At that, I decided I could hang up. My temper was going to be the death of me one of these days, and I tried to blame it on my magic. It was getting antsier and nastier since I had graduated my master classes. My magic needed more challenges, and I knew it. I was itching for another duel after the fiasco at the café.

A few witches looked to me again as I made my way down the stairs. I shook my head and held my hand up, there was nothing I could do for them.

THE CUTE BLONDE jumped around in front of me and swayed her hips provocatively. Music and energy thumped hard around me and made me feel renewed. The music pulsing around me wasn't something that I typically listened to, but I could dig it if the cutie in front of me was into it.

For the life of me, I couldn't remember her name, but tried to keep up with the music. I wasn't much of a dancer, and I was trying my hardest for my new friend. She backed up closer to me and rubbed on me like a cat.

I hated cats and tried to keep my thoughts from that direction, but the more she moved, it was all I could see. I pressed my palm to my magi hanging in the middle of my chest and tried to get my temper under control. There was no need for me to get angry over a girl resembling an animal. It wouldn't have been the first time it had happened. I backed away slowly and made my way through the sweaty teenagers and the drug exchange.

A man that looked to be in his late 30s bumped into me and then gave me a leery smile. He held his hand out to me, and I noticed a little baggie with a few pills inside. I shook my head and kept walking.

Even if I had wanted to get high, my magic would have burned through it quickly, after I had a horrible reaction to it. What we called the essence, protected us. The essence was what kept our magis going. It was the life force to the witches. It was in almost everything in New Orleans. I always thought it was why so many people wanted to come here, besides the alcohol and vampire tours. The essence was addicting and called to all beings, whether or not they knew what it was.

It was probably what had brought Freya here for her little graduation party. I closed my eyes tightly and tried to get her face out of my head. There was a part of me that felt bad for her, a part of me that was curious about her and another part of me that was just damn irritated over her. There were apparently too many parts to me.

When I finally made it to the wall, I was almost disappointed. That was when the paint shooters and powder buckets started to go off at the stage. People surged forward hoping to get drenched in either the colorful goo or the colorful powder. I had been into the thought earlier when I thought of doing it with the cute blonde. But when I saw her in the middle of the floor, I noticed that she had 3 other guys rubbing and touching on her, and I wanted no part of it anymore.

What a waste.

I fought my way back through the crowd and decided that the place wasn't worth it anymore. People were either too high or too into the music to care about anything else. I had come to have some fun company and ended up leaving alone with wasted time. I wiped the sweat from my brow and pushed out of the mass of people and back to the street.

I had apparently gone through the same exit because I had ended up in a dark, dead-end alleyway. I was just about to make it to the street on the other side when a figure stepped in front of me.

"Sterling Masters, what a pleasant surprise." I blinked against the darkness and tried to get a good look at the person talking to me, but it was no use.

I crouched low and got into a defensive stance.

"There is no need for that. I am here to deliver a message."

I didn't move a muscle.

"We want you to bring us Ms. Freya Collette to us, we have been searching for her. I'm sure you know by her nose bleeds." The woman's voice was soft, and I couldn't pick up anything familiar about it.

"I'm not sure I know who you are talking about." I touched my magi on my chest, it doubled in size, reading up for a fight.

"Like hell you don't, flaming red hair, small and delicate with porcelain skin." Her words didn't match the sound of her voice. She didn't sound threatening, but I knew it could change at any moment. Witches were unpredictable. "Take this way, if you don't deliver her to us by Sunday, your coven will suffer. We will find her, whether or not you aide us."

The streetlights blinked on around me, and she was gone. On the way back to the compound, I kept my wits about me but thought on the stranger's words. The only thing that was throwing me off was Freya's last name, it was too familiar.

CHAPTER EIGHT

FREYA

Sterling had disappeared for hours, and my nose had finally stopped bleeding. It made me wonder if he had had something to do with it. I stared at the ceiling and tried my hardest to sleep, but no matter how hard I tried, sleep evaded me. I heard the hushed whispers down the stairs and the stares of all the witches in the hallway when I had walked by. They didn't want me here, and I didn't blame them. I was bringing too much excitement to such a small coven it seemed.

As much as I hated my old life, I found myself wanting to go back to it. These people didn't deserve the issues that I was bringing to them. I had planned on making friends with some of the other witches, but with my constant nose bleed and trying to fix it, not many people wanted to come my way.

I threw the covers off of me in frustration. There was no way I was getting some sleep tonight. Ayre had assured me that everything was going to be fine, but for whatever reason, I couldn't bring myself to believe her. I pulled on some leggings and a robe over my t-shirt and crept out of the room. I left shoes behind, scared they would make noise and crept down the stairs. I took a deep breath, and my magi started to vibrate. When I passed a window, I expected to see my reflection, but there was none. I waved my hands back and forth, but still nothing.

I gulped hard then remembered the vibrating my magi had done. This wasn't too bad. If I was invisible, this could aid me in many things. I shook my head and tried to focus on the task at hand. I could still hear the hushed whispering, and as I got closer, I was relieved I was invisible.

Sterling had returned and was wearing casual clothing, it was odd to see, and Ayre was sitting next to him at the island in the middle of the spacious kitchen. Camey was standing next to a pale man wearing a suit very similar to the ones that Sterling wore. Then I realized they Sterling and the unknown man had the same build and stature and figured he was probably their father. He had his arms folded over his chest and was listening to whatever Sterling was saying. Sterling's eyebrows were pulled together in anger, and his body was ramrod straight. Ayre was watching him with what seemed to be disinterest. I tried to get closer then remembered that I was invisible and almost laughed.

I tried to get as close as possible, but just far enough that I didn't have to worry about them tripping over me or running into me.

Sterling's voice rose in anger. "What do you mean she is staying here?"

His mother gave him a sympathetic look. "We need to protect her. There is more going on here than we realize. If she is Sariah's daughter then we must be careful, her magic will be unmatched."

Ayre nodded her head, in thought. "This explains what happened out in the quarter this morning. It was bizarre, she didn't know what she was doing, it was like her magi was doing it for her."

Their father nodded his head, taking it all in. "There have been cases when that has happened.

Sometimes the magi is more powerful than the witch, it knows what to do to protect their host."

I looked down at the magi on my wrist and touched it affectionately. It had saved my life and was continuing to protect me. I guessed it wasn't so bad after all.

Sterling shook his head. "You don't understand, when the others find out who she is, it's going to be a death warrant. They will throw her to them and not look back."

Camey rolled her eyes. "I trust our coven."

"Not when they start killing people off in your said coven." Sterling's words made dread flood my veins.

What was happening here? What had he discovered?

"You don't have much trust in our people." His father glared at him.

"How am I supposed to? New Orleans covens have been quiet, we have had peace, and now we find out that one of the twins survived and her mother is trying to break free from the Mirror Realm? I'm not okay with this, and I can't imagine how anyone else will be okay with it."

My head spun, and my chest was tight. I felt my

legs give out and my head hit the ground. There was a sharp intake of breath, and someone rushed over and touched my forehead.

Damn, magi.

"What the heck is she doing in here?" Someone said, but I couldn't distinguish the differences in the voices.

"Obviously she knows more about magi than anyone here could have predicted." Sterling's voice was the only one that I could tell apart from the others.

I shook my head against the cold tile. I tried to blink my eyes open but was unsuccessful. My head throbbed, and my stomach was still queasy. Strong arms lifted me from the floor and carried me from the room. Whispers started up again before I lost consciousness.

I BLINKED against the harsh lighting and sucked in a sharp breath as someone touched my tender head.

"It's okay, just healing you up." A soft voice said while the person continued to touch a tender spot. "You had a nasty fall, I heard."

I licked my dry, cracked lips and tried to sit up even though I was blinded by the light above my head. The girl moved back and stopped touching me, and after a few blinks, I could finally see. The girl that had been talking to me stood off to the side next to the wall with her hands behind her back.

"Where am I?" My voice sounded haggard.

"The infirmary, I'll be right back! The Master's wanted me to ring them as soon as you awoke!" She rushed from the room and then came back in with a small phone pressed against her ear. While she talked on it, I had time to observe her. She was a short thing, probably shorter than me and that was saying something. Her blonde hair was pulled back tightly against her skull in a low bun, against the nape of her neck. From what I could tell, she had soft lavender eyes too, but she kept glancing away from me, so it was hard to focus. She had a small button nose that matched her perfectly delicate features and her scrubs were immaculate. They were ironed to perfection, and her white shoes were squeaky clean. I guessed she didn't get much action around her, based on how clean her clothes were.

The room I was in was small with gray walls, and the cot I was sitting on was thin and uncomfortable. I imagined they probably had larger rooms with more comfortable beds for the patients that had to stay for more extended periods of time.

The little nurse finally turned around to me and slipped her phone into the front pocket on her scrubs. "Sterling will be down in a few."

I made a face and went to stand. The floor tried to catch up with my face again, and the petite woman ran forward and caught me, laying me onto the cot once more. She was a lot stronger than she looked.

"The healing process sometimes takes a bit longer for some people. You must ease into it." She tucked a loose strand of my hair behind my ear and gave me a sympathetic smile. "Sterling will help you, I'm sure of it."

I glared at her. "I'm more sure of the fact that he won't."

She chuckled. "He has always been very nice when we have crossed paths."

I made a show of looking her up and down. "Well, of course, he would. You are just his type."

She laughed hard at that. "Every woman is just his type."

"I wouldn't be so sure of that." I whipped my head up at Sterling's amused voice in the corner of the room. He had slipped in unnoticed, and I wondered how much of the conversation he had heard. "Thank you for taking care of her, Leah. I think I can take it from here." Leah departed and left us alone in the room.

"Can you walk?" His voice was deeper when he spoke to me.

"I think so," I went to stand, and dizziness washed over me.

Sterling was quick to my side and helped me support my own weight. We went down a few long corridors before we were outside of the compound. Ayre was sitting on a swing and dismounted when she saw us coming. She ran to me with a look of relief. She pulled me from Sterling's side and hugged me.

"How are you feeling?" She looked me over, head to toe. "You took a really nasty fall."

I nodded my head, worried about what she would say next.

"I'm going to take it you heard everything." Her shoulders slumped, and she looked defeated. Sterling had backed off and had found a chair off in the corner, watching us carefully.

"I don't think so. I don't know who my mother is, what the Mirror Realm is and apparently, I had a twin." I tried to summarize it the best I could, but I was struggling. Everything was still so new, so foreign.

She gave me a small smile. It did little to reassure me. "Do you remember when my mother called you Sariah?"

I nodded, and she continued on, "She called you that because you look just like her. Sariah Collette, she was the previous High Priestess. What happened with you and her is what sent our coven into chaos. The title typically goes down generations. What she dabbled in threw off the New Orleans essence."

"What is the essence?" I asked, picking at my fingernails, nervously.

"It is essentially the lifeblood of the world. It is what helps our magic and the world's magic. Many people call it mother nature. Some places have more of it than others, that is where you will find the supernatural, like us." She looked at Sterling before she went on. "My mother and father are apart of the Council of the Witches, them and the others on the board know what happened that night, the night your mother was banished, and we thought that you and your twin brother was lost."

My head started to spin. It was hard to fathom all of this. I had always imagined finding my birth mother, but now? Not so much. I was afraid to hear more, but I didn't stop her from continuing her story.

"The Mirror Realm is a prison for the supernatural that disrupts the essence in this world, whether by attempting to steal it through dark magic or by murdering masses and achieving it that way. I'm sure there are many other ways to disrupt it, but we aren't taught those things at the academy. Our professors always said that curiosity could lead to a serious downfall. We don't ask questions about it, afraid that they will think we are trying to disrupt the essence." She rolled her eyes as if she didn't approve with this method. I didn't know if I did either.

Knowledge was power but in the wrong hands? It could be detrimental.

She shrugged. "Anyway, it's a dangerous place, and your mother was exiled there." I interrupted her. "Can we not call her that? I don't even know her. How do we even know she is my mother, and what about my father?"

"Sorry," she mumbled. "I don't know anything about him. My parents didn't bring him up last night. But anyway, I guess her people and followers want you back."

She said it so casually like it wasn't a big deal. I imagined it was a lot bigger deal than what she was making it out to be. Sterling was glaring at her, and I figured I was right. I had no doubt that he could hear everything she was saying.

CHAPTER NINE

L eave it to Ayre to spill the beans. I pulled my hands down my face in frustration. Though the Spitfire was taking it a lot better than I had hoped. I kicked my feet up on the table and continued to observe. Every few minutes Freya would glance my way out the corner of her eye, trying to see if I was still here or something. I finally lifted my hand up and saluted her. She was so surprised by my reaction that she whipped back around and didn't look back.

I could still hear their conversation. My magi loved eavesdropping almost as much as I did. The magic allowed their conversation to be played over my magi, almost like an iPod. There was no emotion evident in Freya's voice until Ayre brought up mass destruction. She pushed herself to her feet and shook her head saying, "I will not allow people to be killed!"

A few of the witches hanging out in the courtyard gave her alarmed looks before looking at me with curiosity. I just shrugged like I knew they were having a casual conversation. Ayre followed her out of the courtyard and up to my bedroom. I could hear her throwing her clothes and things into her bag. I scratched my forehead and knew this was time for me to interrupt her rash behavior.

I made my way up the stairs quickly before she could exit the bedroom. I planted both of my hands on either side of the door and gave her my most determined look.

Ayre looked at me and threw herself back onto my bed before she said, "We are really doomed now."

Freya gave me a glare. "Don't try to stop me."

"I really don't want to, in fact, I would love it if you left..." I trailed off and looked at Ayre giving me a death glare even worse than Freya's. "But my sister and mother would literally kill me if I let you leave."

Freya shook her head and dropped her bags to the floor. I thought that she was going to give in and stay. I had thought I had won until she hunched forward in a defensive position, her hands went up into fists to protect her face and her glare got worse.

Of course, it wasn't going to be easy. Who was I kidding?

Ayre dared to start laughing. "You're going to lose."

"I'm not fighting a girl." I planted my feet into the floor even firmer than what they had been before.

"Are you afraid you're going to lose?" She gritted her teeth for emphasis.

"Never, I'm more powerful than you could ever dream to be." I rolled my eyes just as she let her fist fly. It connected with my eye and almost made me fall over, more from shock than pain, but then after a few moments, the pain started to come in with little pinpricks dancing across my face.

Ayre gulped and said, "You forget who her mother is!"

"I am not my mother. I am Freya, my power comes from me and no one else." She went to punch me again, and I was ready, dodged her and it was exactly what she wanted. She picked up her bags and flew under my arm, right through the doorway and down the stairs.

Ayre fell over laughing, clutching her stomach. "Brother, dear brother, you are an idiot!"

I let out a grunt and followed her down the stairs, but I was too late, my father had beat me to her. He held out his hand, and she took it hesitantly. I didn't blame the hesitation one bit, my father was intimidating, to say the least. You could feel his power coming off of him in waves. Sometimes it was hard to be in the same room with him. I couldn't hear what he was saying. My magi hardly stood a chance against my fathers. He knew how to protect himself and continuously had his magi working double time to keep him and his clients safe.

I watched Freya's long red hair bounce as she nodded to him and they turned around and walked back toward me. I could hear him now, "Please ignore Sterling, he can be rather tiresome, but once you get to know him, he will eventually grow on you." He placed her hand in the crook of his elbow and escorted her back up the stairs, but instead of bringing her to my room. He created a whole new place. He touched the ring on his right hand then waved it in front of the wall separating mine and Ayre's room.

No matter how many times I had seen it

happen, it was always shocking to watch. The wall contorted, it turned into what looked to be a wave, falling left then right before it groaned and then separated. It shoved my bedroom down a space and Ayre's before two doors popped up right in the middle. The only thing that distinguished the French doors from mine or Ayre's were the fact that they weren't painted white but were a dark oak. They also didn't have curtains on the inside. I knew the room was going to be empty because that was how mine had been when he had done it for us. He had added hundreds of rooms for the coven and hadn't even blinked an eye. I wasn't sure where the extra space led, but when my mom discovered more rooms, she always brought him to theirs for an excellent long lecture about the Dark Realm and the Mirror Realm. Though I didn't know what those places had to do with the Mortal Realm where we currently resided.

CHAPTER TEN

FREYA

I didn't know why anything surprised me anymore. Apparently, this place was much bigger than what I had thought. The only thing that made sense was, of course, magic. My magi warmed on my wrist at the thought. I stared at Jonathan Masters with a new sense of respect. I could feel the power coming off of him, but at my shock, I almost felt it being pulled back into himself. He touched his right hand before smiling at me.

"I hope that this will be to your liking. You can dress it up or dress it down however you like. It is yours to change at your will." His sophisticated English voice wrapped around me like a warm hug.

I gave him a timid smile and opened up both of the doors. The room was very similar to Sterling's, but the walls were an old shiplap. Jonathan continued to speak, "Go on, make yourself at home. Your magi will know what to do."

With that, he was gone. I closed the doors behind me and sat on the bare wood floor, unsure of what to do with myself. I didn't have anything to help me furnish the new room, and I definitely didn't have money to help. I rested my face on my fist and tried to figure out what he meant by my magi knowing what to do. Ugh, I didn't like riddles or anything I had to think on for far too long. A soft tap on the glass had me turning around and facing the music. Sterling was giving me an irritated look, and I was getting really tired of his better than thou attitude. Though I was pretty happy with my handy work starting to form around his eye.

I folded my arms across my chest and smiled at him triumphantly.

"Is that how you get used to getting your way? Throwing a fit and someone caters to your every need?" His insults were getting worse and worse. At this point, I knew that if I left, it would be because of him. "That's an interesting trait to have being an orphan."

I didn't have time for his rudeness. I didn't have time to be bullied and bossed around by him anymore. There was something wrong with him for him to continually come at me like he was. I tried to keep the tears from spilling over and blinked them back.

I gritted my teeth. "Get out."

He blinked at me like he hadn't expected me to get angry.

I pointed to the door. "I said get out."

I could feel the heat lighting up in my cheeks and wetness falling from my eyes, but I no longer cared. When he finally retreated, I made sure the door was locked before I threw myself down onto my bag and cried.

I DIDN'T KNOW how I had been so exhausted, I was sure it had a lot to do with my emotions being haywire, but it was starting to get out of control. I pushed myself up and off the door, only to let out a shriek at Ayre sitting beside me. She gave me a bashful smile and held her hands up in surrender.

"How did you get in here?" I looked at the doors to make sure they were still locked. Sure enough, they were. I glared at her.

"Locks don't keep witches out. Wards do, but I

respected your privacy for locking the door and climbed through the tiny opening in your closet. It's similar to the one that my brother and I shared, but smaller and I now share it with you instead of him!"

"And you thought that I would be okay with that breach in privacy?" I tried to figure out where she would think this was okay.

"I thought you might be lonely and sleeping on the floor sucks, so I brought you pillows and blankets and an air mattress." She held up the box with the air mattress in it like it was a precious prize. That was when I realized that she had put the blanket over me while I had been sleeping.

"I guess I forgive you now, but next time don't do it." She gave me a very unconvincing nod and then shrugged to add to it.

"I heard what my brother said to you." Her head hung forward, in remorse.

I was unsure of what to say. He hadn't been lying, even though he hadn't been careful about it. But it was okay, I was going to prove him wrong, one way or another that I wasn't to be messed with. I might have been a small little, but that didn't mean that I was missing my fire.

"My entire life, I was alone. I stumbled through every obstacle alone and never had anyone to hold my hand or tell me that I was going to be all right. I just had faith that eventually it would get better, and I would be okay in the end." I pulled the blanket tighter around my shoulders and picked at the frayed edges. "Jumping from one foster home to another, you lose a lot of hope. I was the quiet one, and families don't like the quiet ones. I don't know, never mind." I didn't have the emotional strength to continue.

Ayre grabbed my hand in hers and squeezed it gently. "Whatever happened to you there only made you stronger for here. You aren't alone anymore, and you never have to be alone again. No matter what happens, you always have me, and I might not be enough sometimes, but I will always try to be."

Tears filled my eyes again, and I fought to keep them back. These people had turned me into a big softy. I didn't appreciate it much, but when I looked up, I could see the tears shining in Ayre's eyes too.

CHAPTER ELEVEN

"Y ou didn't! Sometimes I am flabbergasted by your will to hurt others." My father's voice boomed across the library. I flinched as it echoed around me, reminding me of the power that my father possessed.

I took a deep breath and tried to stand up, but the gaze my father pinned on me was enough for me to stay put.

"She is Sariah's daughter, do you know what that means?" He crossed his arms over his chest, stretching his suit jacket tight over his muscles.

"No, but I am very sure you're about to tell me." I sneered.

"It means that when she comes into her full power when her magi allows it, she will be the new

High Priestess." He shook his head like he couldn't believe I hadn't caught on yet.

"What about Mom?" I scratched my head.

"What about her? She has never really filled the role correctly, and she has only been subbing until the real High Priestess came back." He turned away from me and browsed the shelves in front of him. They stretched from floor to ceiling containing the history of our ancestors, along with spells and many books on healing magic.

"This means that you already knew." Of course, he did, my father seemed to know everything that went on in the city, no matter how big or small it appeared.

"Well, of course, I knew Sariah's daughter was alive. I watched her son die and watched her daughter just disappear into thin air. Your mother never came into the full High Priestess power because the essence knew that the real one would come soon." He pulled a book from the shelf and set it on his desk. "I love your mother and your mother is very powerful, but when Freya comes into her power, it will be nothing like you have ever seen before."

"What about Sariah? What do we do about her?"

"Nothing, Sariah is banished, if she were to come back the essence would kill her, and she knows it, though I don't know what she could want with her daughter while she is there." He frowned.

"Finally, something you don't know." And with that, I stormed from the room. My father had always been an ass, the only ones he tolerated was Ayre and my mother, everyone else didn't matter much to him.

Ayre met me at the end of the hall and tried to keep up with my long strides, but I hoped I lost her soon. I didn't have time for her rambling or questions.

"You hate him, but you are just like him." She matched my strides, and her question made me slow for a second.

"If you are here to talk about dad, then you can get lost."

"I'm here to ask you if the training room will be free tomorrow." She was out of breath by the time I made it out to the courtyard.

"You are terribly out of shape." I turned and faced her, leaning against one of the pillars. "That's the only reason I'll free up the gym for you tomorrow."

Her smile was radiant. She nodded her head

and skipped away, not giving me any time to change my mind, and it had me curious, but not for long. I could hear my mother singing in the kitchen and knew she was whipping up something good if she was singing. She only cooked and sang when she was in a good mood, and I wondered what had put her there. There was no way it was Dad, he was in a terrible mood and would possibly ruin anyone's day with just a look. When I saw the thin pastry like rolls on the island my mouth watered.

Crepes.

My favorite and she knew it. I narrowed my eyes at the woman that had given birth to me and tried to figure out what her angle was. She was obviously trying to butter me up. She flipped the mixer on and dumped a little bit of vanilla in it, and I could have died. Mom was making home-made whipped cream to go on top. I spotted the fresh strawberries in the sink and plopped one into my mouth. The fruit burst on my tongue and immediately turned my morning around.

"So, what's all this about?" I stretched my arms wide and leaned against the island in the middle of the kitchen. I couldn't keep my eyes off of the stove as she expertly flipped the thin pastry before she rolled it onto the plate next to the gas stove.

"I want you to stop being so ugly to Freya." There is was. She planted her fists on her hips and turned back toward me.

"I don't know what you are talking about." I avoided looking into her eyes.

"Then just listen. I won't be in the position of power for forever, she will soon take this place, and you will have to answer to her." She filled a crepe with whipped cream and slid it across the granite right in front of me. "Wouldn't you rather her rise to power be a pleasant one or would you rather suffer at her hand?" My mother's eyes grew hard as she looked at my stubborn expression.

"I'm not ready to accept her into this coven." And I wasn't. I didn't understand why, but I couldn't put my finger on it just yet. She didn't belong.

"That poor girl has been alone her entire life. She hasn't belonged anywhere, and you are going to make her feel even more alone." The crepes no longer looked appetizing. I turned away from her and the breakfast. I wasn't hungry anymore.

"She doesn't belong here." I heard my mother set the plate down too hard, angry with my words. "At least not yet."

I TRIED to ignore my stomach growling. I was starving, but there was no way in hell I was going to go back into the kitchen. It probably didn't matter anyhow, all the crepes would be gone. Commotion in the courtyard had me begrudgingly leaving my room to see what the fuss was about. In the middle of the yard, in the air was a cat. It was floating above everyone's head when I saw the orange markings on its stomach and the pink collar, I immediately recognized it as Ayre's cat Freckles. As the animal got higher in the sky, the witches in the courtyard started to back away. My stomach dropped with every foot the cat went up.

I felt like I was going to vomit. I knew what was about to happen and before I could say anything to the growing crowd, Ayre exited Freya's room. Her face went from confused to terror in seconds. She flew down the stairs with her hands over her mouth before she realized that maybe she could save him. She lifted her hands to the sky and chanted. It did nothing, and the cat started to flip before it was stretched at an odd angle, then ripped apart. There were screams from the witches around me, but I couldn't bring myself to utter a single sound. I watched as a piece of paper floated to the ground from the cat's body, that was still hanging lifelessly in the air. Blood splattering the pavement under and around it. The witches scattered, fearful of what was happening.

I picked up the bloody parchment and read what it said to myself.

Bring the girl, or the last thing you have to worry about will be cats.

I swallowed hard and folded up the paper before I tucked it in my back pocket. My mother would need to see it. I could hear Ayre's sobs as I walked to the study and soon after I had made it to the hall, I could hear her screams of sorrow. My sister and I hadn't always gotten along, but her grief made everything terrible. My sister was a lot of things, but she was the happiest person in the coven. She was the light of everything and always cheered everyone up. She was the woman that cared about every living soul, and she was genuine. She was kind, down to her bones.

Me? I was the opposite of her. I didn't care about people until they were useful to me. I didn't want to help others unless I knew that I would get something out of it. I figured I had gotten it from my father, that's why it put me on edge with the way he treated Freya.

Mother wasn't in the study, so I went through each public room that I could find in the compound, there was no way she didn't know what was happening. When I couldn't see her, I decided I needed to head back to the dead cat. Maybe I had missed her there, but instead of Mother, Ayre and Freya were huddled together next to the fallen cat.

Freya looked like she was in deep thought. Her eyebrows were drawn together as she held my sobbing sister. When her eyes met mine, I saw a storm brewing there. I had no idea what she was planning, but I was almost afraid.

CHAPTER TWELVE

FREYA

Sterling watched me carefully, his expression finally moving away from hatred to curious. I didn't know what his deal was, but it was pissing me off to the max. His comments about me being an orphan hadn't been forgotten or forgiven just yet.

Ayre let out a wheezing noise against my chest, and all I could do was rub her back in slow circles. I hadn't had the opportunity to own an animal. Honestly, I hadn't had the chance for much. All I could do was comfort her.

Ayre sniffled loudly, in my ear, before she picked her head up and looked at Sterling. "Do we have any idea who did this?"

Sterling gave her a somber look as he pulled a

folded, bloody piece of paper out of his pocket. He handed it to her and more tears spilled down Ayre's face. She hiccuped, "How could they do this?"

"Who?" I frowned.

Ayre looked down at her lap. "They want you."

"What do you mean?" I pushed myself off of the cobblestone ground and turned on Sterling. I didn't want to know, but unfortunately, I already had ideas forming. My mother's people wanted me, for what, I couldn't imagine. Sterling was staring at me again, but this time with more hatred than before. Of course, I had asked a dumb question.

Didn't we all?

Sterling crossed his arms over his chest and glared at me some more, I didn't know how it was possible, but the skin between his brows just kept getting smaller and smaller. I wanted to touch it and smooth it out, but instead, I made a snarky comment.

"You're going to get premature wrinkles if you keeping looking at me like that." His brows unwrinkled and stretched upon his forehead in surprise.

"I would rather have wrinkles than not have a brain." He rolled his eyes before crouching down next to his sister.

I decided they needed to be alone, but I also

needed to think. I knew there was more on that paper than what they were telling and I wasn't going to pry. I went up the stairs two at a time and closed the door behind me. On the floor was the blankets and pillows Ayre had supplied and right next to it all was my backpack and duffle bag, full of clothes. I could see the sun going down just outside my window and knew my time would be coming soon. I shoved a clean pair of shorts and a t-shirt into the backpack and then changed into a pair of leggings and a tank top. I slid my feet into my converse and threw my hair up on top of my head.

I JERKED AWAKE, angry with myself for dozing off. The sky outside the window was black, and I knew it was my time to run. I didn't want to see anymore suffer because of me. I threw my backpack over my shoulder and pulled my French doors open. The cat and the blood had been cleaned up, and all was quiet in the courtyard.

I tiptoed down the stairs and almost made it to the door on the other side of the vast compound when someone cleared their throat. My head fell back in defeat, and I looked up at the stars, hoping the person hadn't really noticed me.

I was wrong. "Your hair practically glows in the dark." Crap, it was Sterling. Of, freakin', course.

I swallowed hard and turned to face him. "I needed some fresh air, am I a prisoner here?"

He stood up from the swing and cocked his head at me. "I'm not dumb. I know you're going to them. I saw the wheels turning in your mind. I've been waiting for hours for you to make your appearance."

"I don't understand why you are so obsessed with me," I said, matter a fact.

He seemed startled by my words and took a step back, his eyes getting round. "That is definitely not what this is. I'm simply waiting for you to mess up."

"Good for you then, you won't have to anymore." I pulled at a loose strand of hair next to my face.

He shook his head. "You don't realize the danger you are putting the coven in."

"Then why do you care if I stay?" I stepped closer to him, and he took a step back.

"I don't!" We were almost nose to nose now.

"Then let me go." I poked his chest for good measure. "You haven't wanted me here. You wanted me gone the moment you found me in your room."

"You're right about that." He stepped forward, and I scrambled to move backward, so he didn't touch me. "I had hoped you died when you fainted, then my mother would get the High Priestess powers she deserves."

My heart was beating out of my chest, and his words made me falter. I didn't know why I was surprised. Nothing he said should have come as a shock anymore. I nodded my head once, and I was gone.

It didn't take me long to be discovered by my mother's clan, or whoever she was. Walking around the empty Quarter was creepy enough, but to know I was being stalked was even worse. I had heard them when they came running at me, and I even let them hit me over the head. My vision swam, and I felt my legs give out.

I didn't know how long I had been out, but I woke up to my hands being tied behind my back and a bright light in my face. "Welcome back to the land of the living."

"You wouldn't have had to wait if you had just

talked to me. I was coming willingly." I pushed against my binds, looking for a weak spot.

"We couldn't take any chances after what happened the other morning, with one of our most powerful at that." The woman said from behind the light.

I shrugged my shoulders up, uncomfortably and tried to give a toothy smile. "What can I say? I like to do things my way."

"Unfortunately, that's not how this is going to go." When she walked around the light, I could just barely make out her features. Her hair was a deep gray, and her wrinkles on her face were even deeper. The years hadn't been kind to her. I didn't understand though, her voice sounded smooth like honey, but her features didn't match at all. "This is what happens when the essence rejects you. The only way you can perform magic is by your own life force once that happens."

"Why would you continue to use magic?"

"I have been searching for you." She smoothed out her blouse.

"You didn't do that great of a job. It's been that many years since I disappeared?" I tested the binds again. Nothing.

"We had thought you were in New Orleans this

whole time, we were right. We just had to wait for the perfect opportunity, and it arose just a few days ago when your cloaking wore off."

I laughed. "You honestly think that the Jackson Square coven was keeping me hidden?"

She looked at me confused. "Well, of course. How else would you have eluded us this whole time?"

Before I could respond a loud voice boomed across the room, behind the light. "That is enough, Arabella. I am getting tired of the commentary. She eluded you because she wasn't in New Orleans, you twit."

Arabella blanched. "Yes, Your Majesty."

I frowned. What the hell?

"No more of this, I want to see my daughter, bring me to her."

I swallowed again, and my mind went blank before a flood of questions rushed forward. Wasn't she in the Mirror Realm, banished? How was she able to be here in New Orleans? Was I still in New Orleans? Was I ever going to get free? Was my mother cruel and going to kill me?

All the questions vanished as Arabella moved a large mirror to sit in front of me. The bright light clicked off, and the overhead light blinked on.

There in the glass of the mirror was my mother. She didn't look a day over 23. I gazed at her with wide eyes, taking in every single feature I could see. Her thick red hair hung around her face in glossy, thick curls and her lavender eyes weren't as light as the other witches I had met. Her skin was perfect unmarked porcelain, and her figure was small like mine. I looked just like her. Except my hair was much brighter and always had a mind of its own.

"Don't look so afraid daughter," Her eyes softened, and hope blossomed in my chest. Maybe she wasn't so bad after all. "Someone cut the ropes off of my daughter, I want a proper look at her." Two men rushed forward from behind me and sliced the ropes. The material hit the floor with a thud, and I rolled my shoulders and straightened up a bit. My heavy backpack now very much uncomfortable.

"I am not afraid of you or anyone." I scowled at her.

She raised her eyebrows. "Hmmm, you remind me of your father."

I tried to calm my breathing. I had always wondered what my father was like.

"Too bad. I always hated that he didn't comply with my wishes." She narrowed her eyes at me, assessing me once more.

I didn't know what to say. I wanted to stay alive, and I didn't know what these people had in store for me just yet.

"Come closer," She pressed her hand against the glass that separated us and cocked her head, looking me up and down.

I shook my head and stayed rooted in my spot.

She shook her head and laughed. It was beautiful and haunting. "That's fine, we have the perfect thing to make you obey. Bring him in."

I tried to think of everyone that had been at the orphanages with me, anyone that could be used against me, my mind drew a blank.

"My father will make sure that all of you burn. Dammit, I'll make sure that you all burn!" Sterling's voice rang through the room, and my stomach dropped. No.

"This little miscreant was following you around your little escapade," Arabella said as the burly men tossed Sterling down in front of me. His hands were bound behind his back with duck tape, and his legs were bound with rope. His eyes held rage and hatred as he looked me over and saw that I was no longer bound.

"I knew you were working with them!" He shouted. One of the men came forward and kicked him in the stomach, causing him to choke and curl in on himself.

As much as I hadn't liked Sterling, I didn't want him to see pain because of me. It wasn't right.

"Leave him alone, he has nothing to do with this." My mother smiled gleefully as I spoke.

"Come closer, or you will not like the consequences." I was about to ignore her request when I saw a knife materialize out of thin air. Arabella drew the knife down the side of his perfectly sculpted face. Blood beaded up from the cut, but Sterling didn't make a sound.

Even though he didn't do or say anything, I knew he was in immense pain by the sweat forming over his brow. I stepped closer to the mirror, against my better judgment.

"Press your hand against the mirror, right over my hand." I bit my lip. Everything inside of me, telling me not to do it. To die before I did what she said. "The Master's son will suffer if you don't." I turned away from the mirror and watched as Arabella pressed the knife against Sterling's chest. His eyes were the only thing that gave him away.

"Fine, but please let him go when I do. He has nothing to do with this or us. I personally can't stand the fool.

My mother narrowed her eyes at me again. "Interesting. Yes, we shall leave him be." Arabella took a step back to solidify the woman's statement.

I was just about to press my hand against the glass when Sterling spoke. "Have her swear on her magi." A kick to the stomach was his reward, but I appreciated it and had her do so. Sterling watched as my mother swore on her magi with gritted teeth. He nodded once when she did it correctly. I pressed my hand on the glass and was ripped from the world I called home.

The air was stolen from my lungs, and I felt like I had taken a trip through a vacuum. I could hear an echoing yell, but my mind and eyesight was too foggy to register it. When my brain felt back to normal, I sat up and knew I wasn't in Kansas anymore. The sky was yellow, and the grass underneath me was a soft blue. There was a cracked mirror laying in front of me, and I knew exactly where I was. The damned woman had somehow traded my spot with hers in the Mirror Realm. Though I wasn't sure why it was even called that. Everything around me wasn't a mirror of the earth at all. I kicked the broken mirror and looked around me.

My magi warmed against my wrist, and I had

small comfort that I would have it with me. I was standing in a big field with fluffy purple flowers randomly popping from the grass. I felt like I was in a Dr. Seuss book. When I got close enough to pluck a flower free, it swung my way and jabbed into my hand. The little fluff was actually a spike ball. I let out a hiss of pain and jumped out of the way.

"They don't like new people." I whirled around at the small voice, but nothing was there. I took a deep breath and tried to steady myself. "Don't be frightened. I won't try to hurt you."

I squinted my eyes, and there it was. More like, there she was. A tiny fairy about the size of my fingernail. She had brown hair piled on top of her tiny head, and the outfit she wore was an iridescent blue. Her little wings were a blur as she floated in front of me.

"Oh hi," This was great, fairies were real too. What else was I going to find out? What else was real?

"Though my magic is great, I will not harm you." She landed in the grass and almost disappeared, her dress blending in perfectly.

"How do I know?" I crossed my arms over my chest.

"You have no idea about the place you have

fallen into, you are trapped here, and you have no one else. Trusting me is your only option." She placed her hands on her hips and smirked.

"Fine, but I don't completely trust you." I crossed my arms over my chest. A big gust of wind decided to blow through at that moment and knocked me off of my feet. I blinked hard and tried to stand up, but the wind hit me back down again.

I had expected the little fairy to be long gone, but instead, her eyes were white, and she was rooted in place. She smiled at me, and it was terrifying, her brown hair wiping around her head wildly. She was the epitome of fierce.

CHAPTER THIRTEEN

STERLING

J ust as Sariah stepped through the mirror and Freya was sucked through, someone hit me over the head. She had risked her life for mine. As I blinked my eyes open and rubbed my sore head, I was thankful that they had sworn on their magis or I wouldn't have survived. Then I remembered the mirror that Freya had been sucked into and I rushed to the other side of the room.

All that was left of the mirror were sharp jagged edges and no magic left. I pulled my shirt over my head and carefully picked up all the pieces of glass, making sure I didn't miss any. I didn't know if it was possible, but I needed to bring the mirror to the compound.

When I reached my home, the doors were open wide, and a large gathering was in the garden. My mother had just finished talking, and when her eyes flashed to me, I could see a fury there like I had never seen before. Mumbling and whispers flew around me as the witches dispersed to their rooms or left to go to their homes. I ignored it all, all I could think of was the glass in my hands.

"Where have you been? I have been worried sick!" My mother stormed my way.

I placed the broken mirror on the table and hung my head. If I hadn't been such an ass, none of this would have happened. "I'm so sorry." I didn't usually apologize, and the words hurt coming from my lips.

My mother must have noticed my lack of clothing, and her eyes narrowed. "I was worried that Sariah had harmed you in some way. I couldn't find you."

I closed my eyes and recounted my almost death. "So you know she escaped?"

She looked to her magi hanging low on her neck before she nodded. "Yes, I felt the power leave me and figured it had been Freya, but then I couldn't find Freya anywhere, and I knew."

"I followed her." I hung my head again.

"How did you know she was going to leave?" Sadness filled my mother's features.

I tried to think of the best way to say it. "I pushed her to go."

The sting of her hand on my face had me blinking, though I wasn't surprised. I had deserved it. My mother had never lifted her hand to me before, but this time, it was justified. I waited for her to yell, but all she did was start pacing in front of me.

"What happened?" Disappointment had replaced her sadness.

I closed my eyes against it before I spoke. "Sariah used Freya to get out. Like she swapped places with her through the mirror."

My mother let out a gasp and went toward the doors like she could do something to rewrite the past. "I was afraid of her finding a loophole. We need that mirror! She didn't take it, right?"

I picked up a piece of it and held it out to her, with shaking hands. "She broke it."

My mother's face fell, and she looked like she was going to collapse. In a few seconds, she aged tremendously before my eyes. "We must bring it to your father, there may be a way to fix this."

When I picked up the glass again, I felt hope, not much but it was enough. I had wronged Freya, and because of that, I was the reason New Orleans was now doomed. I didn't know much about Sariah, but I knew her rule wasn't going to be a good one.

My father threw a glass globe across the room, and I stood stoic as it burst into thousands of little pieces. "Do you know what you have done?" The man that was usually calm and collected was losing it.

I nodded my head, unsure of my voice. The man had never cared for me much, and I was giving him even more ammunition against me.

"I don't think you do. Your mother no longer has the High Priestess power. She can't protect this coven any longer. She can't protect you or your sister against the madness that has been unleashed in our city." He raked his fingers through his hair and caused it to stand up. "The witches ruled this city, but I am afraid with Sariah back in power, other creatures will start to come from their shadows."

I looked at the worn wooden floors and shook

my head. "What about our people? What will happen to them?"

My father took my mother's hand in his and kissed it softly. "Some will leave and join her, some will stay."

"How do we get them to stay?" Ayre asked, clutching her hands to her chest.

"We have to show them that we are still a powerful family." My mother lifted her head high, ready for the challenge that was to come.

"What about Freya?" My eyes flicked to the broken mirror on my father's desk.

Ayre's head wiped in my direction, and she narrowed her eyes at me. "What about her? You are the one that pushed her away, you are the reason we are in this mess, to begin with!"

"If you hadn't brought her here, she would have gone back to where ever it is that she is from." Fury laced my words.

"Foster care?" She flew from her seat and got within inches of my face. She lifted her hands up like she was going to strangle me before she let out an exasperated sound and stormed from the room. I winced at her words. I had been cruel in how I had treated Freya and guilt was eating me up because of it. I didn't normally feel this way, but I now realized how wrong I had been.

Heck, I could have even gotten along with her if I had stopped being a jerk and yet, she had still sacrificed herself for me.

My mother scowled at me. "How did she end up in the mirror, to begin with? Why would she trade places with Sariah?"

"They were going to kill me." My mother gasped and put her hand over her mouth.

"Why would she sacrifice herself for you? You are lucky she did, if I had been in her shoes, I would have let you perish." My father shrugged his shoulders. "Karma is alive and well within the essence, and you are lucky that Freya is merciful."

I nodded my head solemnly as my family started to make preparations for keeping the coven together. I couldn't focus on their words, so I stood up and left the room.

THE MUSIC PULSED around me and I knocked back another shot. Alcohol did nothing, but make my mind foggy, my magi continually trying to work off its effects. I was sure if my magi had a soul and a body, it would have been more than pissed at me and the way I was acting. All I could see was Freya falling into the mirror. I kicked back another shot, the burn of the alcohol leaving a trail down my throat. I shook my head and let out a war cry, and the girls next to me squealed.

This was a new bar, but the women were all the same. It didn't matter what you looked like when the vodka flowed. It didn't matter how you acted as long as you flashed the money. The girls were all the same. All of them, but Freya.

Another shot.

I couldn't think about her. I had lost her, and there was nothing I could do to bring her back to our realm. My magic wasn't powerful enough. Now that my mother had lost her High Priestess powers, no one could bring her back except Sariah, and I needed to accept that for what it was. If she put her there, she probably wasn't going to bring her back. The woman was evil.

The blonde next to me snuggled in closer and purred something provocative in my ear, and I expected the desire to be the outcome, but instead, nothing happened. The bartender watched me carefully, probably waiting for me to fall over from all the alcohol I had consumed. I had lost count how many shots I had taken, and I still felt nothing, but a headache and a small amount of growing aggravation. The blonde rubbed her hand up my thigh, and I grabbed her hand immediately and flung it away from me. She pouted, and that was usually the thing that got me, I had always liked a pouting, begging woman. The submission was something that got me, but not tonight. These women were nothing. I slammed a hundred dollar bill on the bar and slid it toward the woman handing out more alcohol. I pushed away from the remaining woman and made my way to the door. There were more women in the bar tonight than men, and the women were starting to become desperate.

They writhed and ground against each other, making a show for the men at the bar, trying to lure them in. I rolled my eyes and shoved them out of my way. When I finally made it out to Bourbon, I had an odd sense of de ja vou. The humidity stuck to my skin, and the smell of cigarettes floated around my head. Drunken men and women stumbled from the other bars around me and sung off key. One man stumbled into me, I helped right him and thought it was by accident until he grinned up at me and his eyes were clear. His teeth had golden caps on them and were sharpened into points. His light bronze skin was slick with sweat, and his eyes were a deep purple.

I pushed him away from me, but he grabbed my arms and pulled me closer. "Sariah wants you. She wants her mirror back."

I shoved him again, this time putting a little magic in my force and he flew across the street away. A few people gasped and ran, but it was more a stumbling action than anything, and I wasn't worried about their drunk accounts. No one had recorded it, so I wasn't concerned. Plus it was New Orleans after all, it wouldn't be the first time that something had been posted on the internet that didn't make sense to humans. New Orleans was full of magic and soul, and that's why people came to visit in the first place.

The man growled at me. "She will have you. Sariah is impatient, but she is powerful. She will get what she wants."

Before I could say anything back, he disappeared into thin air. Chills traveled up my spine and goosebumps lit up my arms. Something wasn't right.

CHAPTER FOURTEEN

FREYA

The fairy led us to the forest, quickly. She kept looking over her shoulder as she flew, muttering under her breath. Terror was unwinding in my gut, and I refused to glance back, afraid of what I would see. The trees were white and reminded me of birch, but they were much thicker and dense. They were like albino pine trees.

When we were far enough into the forest, the fairy started to fly up one of the trees, encouraging me to follow her. I looked at how far apart the limbs were and offered up a prayer that I would make it up the tree. By the time I made it halfway up, my hands were raw, and my feet were sweating. I was thankful for my converse and stamina. My breath was coming out a bit faster, and my heart rate was steadily climbing. I didn't know if I would make it to the top of the tree and that was where the tiny mythical creature was heading.

I grasped the small branches and held on for dear life. There was no doubt that if I fell, I wouldn't survive. The fairy perched on the branch in front of me and pulled at the pastel pink leaf floating next to her face.

She pulled at it nervously before she looked me in the eye and smiled. "That was a close one."

I closed my eyes, and all I could think was ignorance was bliss. That I really didn't need to know what was behind us.

"Your sister got out, then?" She crossed her arms over her chest.

"My sister?" I wrinkled my eyebrows. "Oh, right! No, that was my mother."

The fairy's eyes got big, and she took a step back like I had hit her. "She used her own daughter to get out?"

I shrugged my shoulders. "I don't know, I'm sure you know her better than I do. I just met the woman."

"No, I don't. I stay far away from the ones that

are exiled here. The black magic they use changes them, and you can feel it when you get close."

"What do you mean, black magic?" I asked.

"Blood rituals, blood drinking, human sacrifice, the like." She shrugged like it wasn't a big deal. "They're like vampires, but they have a little sliver of a soul left, unlike the vampires who have nothing. You can always see it in the eyes, they're empty."

I nodded my head and looked down the trunk of the tree expecting to see a monster waiting for us at the bottom, but there was nothing there.

"You won't see it, it was the magic. But if you don't escape it in time, it'll suck you dry." She shivered hard.

"How did my mother escape it?" I asked, scared of the answer.

"She created it." The fairy looked down at the ground again. "Anyway, I forgot to introduce myself, I'm Wyna."

"I'm Freya," I shivered and crossed my arms over my chest as if I could get rid of the chill that had wrapped its way around my body.

"How do I get out of here?"

Wyna squinted at me, concentrating hard. "You weren't exiled here, I don't see why you couldn't leave, but your portal disappeared as soon as you came through, so I don't know." She looked away from me before she squinted off into the distance.

"Can you tell me more about this place? Why is it called the Mirror Realm?" I leaned against the slender trunk and looked off into the distance too. All I could see were mountains above the tree line and then over the mountains was thick, white clouds.

She shrugged before crossing her ankles. Her little wings doing all the work to keep her body upright. "I'm not very old, but this is one of the first magic realms. They say that all magical beings were created here before they were sent to other places." She twirled her hands around like she was conjuring magic. "Then there were problems with these beings, and because of this, the people from other realms thought it was fitting to send them back here."

"If they were created here, then does that mean that there are more creatures out here?" I looked down at the blue forest floor.

"Yes, and no." She gave me a haunting look. "These are the barren lands. The magical rejects had to go somewhere. The mist was created for a reason, it was made to keep the creatures here that are banished, your mother made it different, changed it."

"Leave it to good ole mom," I muttered under my breath.

I had always imagined meeting my mother or father and them telling me that it was for me to have a better life, or that they knew they couldn't take care of me or something like that. I never imagined my mother being an evil witch with a vendetta over New Orleans.

"She made it benefit herself. That's why this is the baron lands now. No creatures can live here, and it honestly helped the kingdoms more than anything, they didn't have to worry with the banished anymore, so they let your mother live as long as she stayed out of their way. Now she's gone, and here you are." She blew out some air and gave me a nervous glance.

"So, what are you doing here if this is the baron lands?" I asked, suspiciously.

"I was sent here to keep an eye on Sariah. We felt the void open and thought there had been a new banishment, they sent me immediately to investigate. I witnessed you taking her place." Wyna scratched at her forehead.

"What does this mean for me?" I considered

running. I didn't want to be stuck here, but I wasn't so sure about visiting the nearby kingdoms either.

"I am not entirely sure. You aren't banished here, you aren't a prisoner. You'll most likely be honored as a Royal Guest." Wyna clapped her hands in front of her, excitement taking over her features before going somber once more. "But we have to hurry, we can't risk the magic coming back for us."

WE WEREN'T as quick going down the tree as we had gone up and when I say we, I really meant myself. Wyna just slowly floated beside me, acting as if she was really contributing to the long climb down.

I ran across the clearing with Wyna flying at my shoulder. Eventually, she broke away from me and flew faster, I couldn't keep up, but was doing my damnedest to try to. She led me to a path that looked like it would go through the mountains before she stopped and laughed.

"I don't know why we are doing this the hard way," She giggled, and I watched as a bubble surrounded us. When the bubble started to lift us off the ground, my stomach dropped. I wished she had conjured up some handles while she had been at it.

At least she had wings.

I took a deep breath and tried to calm myself as we rose higher and higher into the air. Eventually rising up even higher than the peaks of the mountains. Then as we started to go through the clouds, I could see the steeples on the top of what looked to be a castle, its gray bricks giving me an ominous feeling in the pit of my stomach. I had always imagined there being homes around the palace where peasants lived, but as the clouds cleared, there was no such thing here. There was a thick wall that surrounded the structure and archers sitting on the top. I almost shouted to Wyna when I realized they couldn't even see us.

As we passed over their heads, I could make out their features. They had long, pointed ears and almond-shaped eyes. They had thin cords of metal going through the tips of their ears, and most of their faces were adorned in piercings of all shapes and sizes.

Wyna broke my fixation on them when she started to talk. "That's the elven kingdom, they don't like witches or many other creatures in this realm. They believe witches to be the problem to all things. They are miserable beings, truly."

That explained the feeling I had.

We passed over a field very similar to the baron lands except this one was full of different colored horses. I rubbed my eyes, unsure of what I was seeing. But sure enough, they were unicorns. Their irredcent horns reflecting the sunlight as the galloped about.

"I forget you're from earth, where most magical beings are extinct. Here they are wondrous and most run free." She gazed down at the beasts with admiration.

More trees passed below us before we finally started to descend on another kingdom, but there was no way it was possible. We had just passed the elves. I looked back behind us, to find the steeples of the haunting castle gone.

Wyna waved her hands around like she had read my mind. "Oh, right. You also don't know about bubble travel. It's a lot faster than you would think. We have traveled at least 700 miles."

It felt like the bubble popped from beneath me. I tried to regain my footing at her admittance. "We have hardly been traveling for an hour."

She shrugged her shoulders. "Magic."

Right, the explanation for everything.

Farmland spread far and wide beneath us for many miles, or what I thought to be before I could finally see the next castle. My eyes widened in shock. It was made of what looked to be unicorn horns, iridescent glass. It was everything from my childhood, it was magnificent.

"Don't get too impressed, the king slaughtered many to build his empire." I didn't think we were going to be stopping here at those foreboding words, but much against my intuition, we started to come to a stop. The bubble dropped to the ground and POP, it was gone. Leaving behind the smell of cotton candy. The wall around the castle wasn't as big as the elve's, but it was more terrifying. Spike protruded from the top of it, and the outside of it had red dripping down the sides, like blood.

I gulped hard.

"Yes, it's real blood. The castle's magic keeps it here to remind the people of what happens when there is rebellion and war. It's a constant and almost fresh reminder each day." I cringed as she continued on like this was normal. But maybe it was... "Don't worry, Queen Armia had no say in the matter, it was all her father, and he is very much gone and dead."

I felt my shoulders sag in relief. People milled around us, trying to get to their jobs or their families. Children ran around the streets, their skin and hair even brighter than the grass and dirt under my feet. I quickly moved to follow Wyna and heard a shriek. I stopped immediately and looked around me. Everyone seemed to be moving about normally, like they hadn't heard a thing, except for Wyna, who had her fists planted on her hips. She pointed down, and I noticed a fairy family there.

I could have rolled my eyes, but I didn't want to be the rude one in a new realm. I didn't need to make enemies early on. I didn't know how long I was going to be stuck here.

My foot was right next to them, and I realized that I had almost stepped on them. But what the heck were they doing in the middle of a crowded, busy street? I quirked an eyebrow at them and tried to watch my feet as Wyna started off again. And as I paid attention to my feet, I discovered more creatures and species than before. The streets were alive with activity and excitement. There were colorful witches on the corner performing cheap magic tricks. I guess there were still those in magical realms.

As if Wyna reread my mind, she scoffed at the

man and rolled her eyes. "Cheap thrills. He probably has no magic and has been shunned from his community. The poor will do anything around these parts."

We continued farther into the kingdom, and I couldn't help but stare at everything happening around me. The vendors set up with local produce, that affirmed that I definitely wasn't in Kansas anymore. There were countless food stations and long lines in front of them. As hard as I had been staring, I didn't realize that I was being gawked at too. I gulped. As more people turned to me, it seemed like the entire kingdom had eyes on my every movement.

We pushed through the growing crowd surrounding us, and Wyna turned back to me, flying backward. "Don't let them bother you, you are the first outsider in many years. Well, actually," She crossed her arms over her chest and became thoughtful. "You are the first in probably hundreds of years besides the prisoners in the barren lands."

It didn't make me feel any better. But I didn't know why I was the focus of attention, there were white skinned people milling around. Wyna answered my thoughts again. "It's your clothes."

Then I realized, of course, everyone was

dressed like it was the Middle Ages here. The women wore long dress, and though they were bright and beautiful, they wouldn't have fit in where I came from. The fairies flying around were the skimpiest. They had tube tops and tiny shorts or skirts, their feet bare. The men wore leathers, and many had weapons strapped to their hips.

Besides the fairies, I was in rather revealing clothing. There were many long glances and smirks thrown my way. I swallowed hard and focused on the ground in front of me.

When we got to the large castle gates, Wyna turned to me. "Don't say anything. The people here know me, they don't know you."

CHAPTER FIFTEEN

STERLING

I paced the floor of my her bedroom. I winced at the blankets piled high and the pillows shoved up against the wall. Her clothes were folded neatly on top of her suitcase and guilt was taking over me again.

I had come to Freya's room to help ease the bad emotions that had taken my body hostage. It was useless. Nothing was going to work, especially with all the glares my family kept throwing my way. I growled in frustration and slammed my palm into the wall. At the same time my hand connected with the drywall, the ground began to shake, and the wall trembled under my hand. I jumped away in surprise. I knew it hadn't happened because of me. I knew I hadn't been the one to start a minor earthquake. I was more in control of my emotions than that, or at least, I hoped.

I rushed to the window when I heard car alarms going off. The ground continued to shake, and I wondered if the building was going to go down. Lights started flickering on in nearby buildings and businesses. My eyes flicked over the surrounding area, watching for movement or anything to give away what this was. That was until I noticed a building going down in the distance. It looked like it was going down in the business district where many of the hotels were. Dust and rubble clouded the air. The ground and compound stopped shaking, and I had a sinking feeling in my gut.

It wasn't an earthquake at all. It was Sariah. I didn't know how I knew, but there was no doubt about it. Everything had been quiet.

I could hear my mother speaking down the hall and wondered how panicked she was. I doubted that she knew what was happening. I rushed from Freya's room and directly to my mother, checking on a family a few rooms down from ours. She shook her head when she saw me. She must have seen the knowing look in my eye, and she didn't want to cause panic. She assured the family before closing the door behind her.

She put her hand on my elbow and led me to my bedroom. Her hair was up in a towel, and she was barefooted, which wasn't a normal occurrence. Though she was easily frazzled and a little panic driven at times, her appearance was always put together. I couldn't tell the last time I had seen her with her hair in a towel, I had probably been just a child.

Her wide eyes searched mine when she pulled me to a stop. "What do you know?"

"I saw a building go down in the distance, it was a rather large one." I raked my hands through my hair before I continued on. "I would imagine the earth shaking was her bringing in enough power from the essence to take down the hotel or whatever it was."

My mother almost looked like she relaxed. "Sariah." She shook her head and crossed her arms over her white t-shirt. "We should have known that she was going to come back with a bang. It has been too quiet for days."

"Has Father figured anything out about the mirror?" It was all I could think of, even now. My grief and guilt driving me to do whatever it took to make this right.

"No, though you did collect all the pieces. It will

take a lot of power to restore it and even then, we don't know if anything has happened to her there." My mother gave me a sad smile, I knew she could feel my torment, but I didn't want to focus on it with her.

"What do we know about the Mirror Realm?" I asked, determined to find a way around the mirror.

"It is where we came from, or rather our ancestors. All magical beings are from there. The reason it is called the Mirror Realm is because that is the only way to get there. It has been our dumping ground for prisoners for ages, though I don't know much else. All magical beings are from there, remember that before you do something stupid."

She knew me too well and knew that I was going to do whatever it took, even if it meant traveling somewhere I wasn't familiar with. I didn't know the land, but I did know that I was powerful and had harnessed my magic at a young age, not much frightened me. Not even magical beings.

I SAT PERCHED on the roof of the compound, not able to sleep. I watched in the distance, waiting for another building to crumble to the streets of our city. There was a growing fear inside of my chest that they would come for us next. I shook my head, trying to clear the growing unease settling in. I backed away from the ledge and put my face in my hands, there was only so much guilt a person could experience.

Just as I was about to head in for the night, I watched as lights and wind swirled in the distance. Magic circled around the area that had lost its building, and I observed as a new one started to grow into the sky. Vines carried the largest pieces of brick and began to rebuild the structure crudely. I was afraid of what this would do to the humans until I noticed the iridescent bubble surrounding it all. The humans wouldn't know. They probably hadn't even known about the building going down in the first place. I could have slapped myself.

Of course, Sariah would take such measures. She didn't need anyone harping on her plans or ruining them before she even got started. I took the stairs two at a time and about ran head first into my father. He steadied me by my shoulders and looked into my eyes.

He smiled then, and I had a strange feeling of dread coat my body. Then he started to speak. "We found her."

I was dumbfounded, but I didn't know why. I should have known that if anyone could do it, it was my father. He led me down the hallway straight to his office, the mirror was sitting up on his desk, and the lights were low. He waved his fingers forward and the mirror illuminated. I tentatively took a step forward. My heart skipped a beat when my eyes landed on her. Her red hair was in long tatters down her back, and her face was smudged with dirt, but that wasn't what had me staring.

It was the fact that she was about to enter into a massive castle with a fairy on her shoulder. Her light eyes were bright with wonder as she took her surroundings in and the fairy spoke adamantly as they made their way through the dark corridor. Just as I was about to ask my father something, Freya turned her head sharply and looked directly into my eyes. She furrowed her brow and frowned, before shaking her head and continuing on.

For a second, I could have sworn she was seeing me, but I didn't know how that would have been possible. My father was looking at me with a curious grin and a cocked eyebrow. I let out the breath I didn't realize I had been holding and cleared my throat.

"How is it possible that we can see her? Does

that mean that she will be able to come back through?" I asked.

He shook his head. "She has left the banished lands, any hope for bringing her back through this mirror is lost."

My eyes found their way back to the girl with the flaming hair. Somehow, the annoyance that I had had with her had turned into something else. It had evolved into a different kind of curiosity with much less animosity than before.

"How did she get out of the banished lands?" I asked, my voice taking on a different tone. A softer one.

"That is an interesting question, now isn't it? It seems to me that our sweet Freya is quite resourceful." My father turned away from me and left the room.

Indeed she was.

CHAPTER SIXTEEN

FREYA

The hair on the back of my neck prickled and I got the strangest feeling that I was being watched. When I turned my head to look back, nothing was there; but I couldn't shake the feeling that something had been. Wyna continued to prattle on about the castle and the royalty that lived here. She had taken up residence on my shoulder, and as much as I didn't mind it, the little thing had a voice that carried. I found myself wincing more than I meant to.

When we finally made it to the throne room, I paused. I had never met royalty before. I had never met anyone really important. Bouncing around from foster home to foster home didn't exactly give a fun or adventurous life. I didn't know how to act, and the only royalty or important people I had ever encountered had been on my tv. Wyna looked up at me startled.

"What is it? Does my breath stink?" She looked around horrified. Like anyone could smell her little breath.

I let out a small laugh at her comment. "No, I just don't know what to do. I have never been around anyone famous or important before."

It was Wyna's turn to laugh. "There is nothing to be afraid of Queen Armia is wonderful."

I believed her, but it did nothing to calm my erratic heart. I took a deep breath and took a step forward. The walls were gold and silver. It seemed to be dripping off of everything. But the throne, it was made of wood. It was a large wooden chair and seated right in the middle of it was a woman with lavender eyes and long raven hair. Her legs were dangling over the side of the throne, and her eyes twinkled with mischief. Her voice boomed around us, "Welcome back, Wyna! Welcome newcomer, I am Armia! Welcome to the kingdom of Arbor."

A man cleared his throat beside her, "Queen Armia," he corrected. I didn't know how I had missed him in my observation of the room, but I couldn't seem to take my eyes off of him now. His purple eyes were a touch lighter than Queen Armia's, and his light blonde hair was cropped to his shoulders. He had his arms crossed over his chest and was looking at the queen with disapproval.

The queen rolled her eyes and glanced at him over her shoulder. "Really, brother, you know I loathe the title."

The prince pressed his lips together in a tight line and looked to his pointed shoes. Queen Armia went to stand as we got closer and I noticed that the blouse she was wearing was actually a crop top and her pants were skin tight. A jewel twinkled above her belly button as she moved about. Her brother stayed standing right where he was, choosing to keep looking at the ground in front of him.

Wyna flew from my shoulder and crashed into Queen Armia's arms. The queen let out a spell of laughter and clutched her to her breast. Wyna floated up to her body before taking a seat on the queen's shoulder. The woman smiled at me, and I had the urge to bow. I leaned forward slightly, and Queen Armia grabbed my shoulders to keep me from going any farther.

"You have come here as a friend to Wyna, then you are a friend to me. No need to bow."

"Yes, Your Majesty." I couldn't help it. I had watched Disney growing up.

"Please, just call me Armia." She gestured over her shoulder. "This is my brother, Cal." He chose to nod his head and continue to look at the ground. They didn't have many similarities between them.

"I'm Freya." I didn't know what else I could possibly say.

Armia took a step backward and fell gracefully into her wooden throne. "What has brought you so far, Freya?"

"My mother," I paused, not really sure of where I should start. "She was banished in the barren lands."

"Was?" Armia wrinkled her eyebrows. I watched her brother out of the corner of my eye, he didn't move.

"Yes, she used me to escape." It was my turn to look at the floor.

Armia sat up straighter and narrowed her eyes. "You speak of Sariah."

I swallowed hard and nodded my head.

"I had feared as much," She bit the inside of her lip. "Now you are trapped here."

"Seems that way, yes. I wouldn't know how to get home even if I wanted to." My words surprised us both.

She raised her eyebrows and Wyna leaned forward with a concerned look on her face. "I will have Wyna fill me in on your journey, but why wouldn't you want to leave? You haven't been here long."

"As much as I love my realm, I wonder if this is my fate, to start over here." I didn't know where any of this was coming from, but I continued on anyway. "I wouldn't know where to start back there, I think I could do a better job here. Where people would have a chance at getting to know me and maybe I wouldn't be that much of an outsider."

Armia leaned back in her chair and addressed me cooly. "You will be an outsider here, yes, but my people will accept you. Are you sure that you want to stay? You don't want to follow your mother and go back to your home?"

"I have no home there. And the woman you call my mother? She is no such thing. All she did was give me life and then tried to take it back." I tried not to let too much hatred sink into my words.

Armia looked down at Wyna on her shoulder and frowned. "If you wish to stay, no one will stop you," She smiled then. "And it's always nice to have an earth dweller here every once and awhile. It's nice to get caught up on the times."

I nodded my head forward. Cal still hadn't looked up from the floor.

"You will stay at the castle, of course, you are a royal guest, and until we find out your powers and your ranking in society around here, you will keep me company throughout your stay." Armia clapped her hands. "Cal will show you to your rooms."

Cal finally looked up from the floor and scowled at the queen. "I am no errand boy."

She rolled her eyes. "I know this, I just figured you would like to get to know our guest a little better. You haven't spoken once since she came in, that is very unlike you."

Cal frowned. "I am allowed to hold my tongue on your behalf."

Armia lifted a perfectly sculpted eyebrow. "Very well, but you will still show her to her rooms."

THE WALK through the halls was quiet. We had two guards flanking us, and it made my hackles rise, though I understood why they were there. The prince's life was important, and they couldn't risk that. Not for some silly outsider that was wearing odd clothes. Cal was wearing a sleeveless tunic that fell right above his knees and tight pants like Armia's. They reminded me of leggings, and then his low cut pointed weird shoes. His arms were covered in thick olive colored tattoos, and his entire presence intimidated me.

We paused at a set of double doors, and Cal turned to face me. "Please don't leave your room without me or my sister. Wynn is great and all, but she's the size of a baby carrot, and I would hate for something to happen to you before I got to know you." Cal looked up at me bashfully under thick eyelashes.

My stomach did a flip-flop. "Um, right of course." I hated how I stammered when I was nervous.

"Rest easy, Ms. Freya." He bowed low before smiling up at me, his straight white teeth gleaming at me in the dimly light hallway. "I have no doubt we will see more of each other."

My thundering heart probably followed him all the way down the hall. I floated into the lavish set of rooms and threw myself onto the fourposter bed situated in the middle of the room.

"It's nice to finally have a man be nice to me,

rather than hating me every second of the day," I muttered to myself before I decided it was time to explore my living conditions.

CHAPTER SEVENTEEN

STERLING

nger was fizzling right under the surface. Who was that guy and who did he think he was? Ignoring her then flirting? I rolled my eyes at the scene playing through the mirror. Freya's words had me snapping my attention back to her on the bed.

"It's nice to finally have a man be nice to me, rather than hating me every second of the day." She closed her eyes tightly before she looked around herself.

Remorse filled every inch of me. I had no doubts that she was speaking about me and how terrible I had been to her. I watched as she oohed and awed over her surroundings and rightfully so, but I didn't understand why she would want to stay there. Living in a castle did have its perks, but did she really hate us that much to not want to come back? I understood why she wouldn't want to come back because of me, but what about my sister and parents? Hadn't they left enough reason for her to want to stay?

A shuffling noise startled me out of my thoughts, and I looked up to find Ayre standing in the doorway. She looked around me and eyed the full-length mirror, not a scratch to be found on it, thanks to our father's magic. She frowned at me like I had been caught doing something forbidden. Or maybe it was forbidden to be watching Freya like I was...

"Father did it? Can we get her back?" Ayre made slow movements toward me, almost hesitant.

"What if she doesn't want to come back?" I asked, not looking at her.

She marched around me and stood directly in my line of sight. "What do you mean, she doesn't want to come back?" She narrowed her eyes at me, accusingly.

"I don't know, that's just what she told the queen there." I covered my face with my hands, waiting for her to physically attack me.

"This is all your fault! All of it! I don't know

why you were so hell-bent on hating her, but here you go! You have pushed one of my only friends away and probably the only one that could defeat her mother. Do you realize what you have done?" Ayre's voice was shrill, taking on a strange lilt as she continued on.

When I lifted my head up to look at her, I noticed her hair floating around her head like a halo and I knew she was on the brink of losing her magic. I needed to talk her down.

"I know that, okay? I know that I screwed up. I don't know why I did it. Maybe it's the fact that I feel pulled toward her and it's the most annoying thing I have ever experienced. Maybe it's the fact that I can't go out and have a good time without thinking of her red hair or her fiery personality that matches it?" I let out a grunt and spun away from the feisty woman facing me in the mirror. She was brushing her teeth, and her hair was pulled up on top of her head, and she looked adorable. This was terrible.

Ayre just stared at me with her mouth hanging open. "Who are you?"

I rolled my eyes. "I know I am not making a lick of sense, but I have been pushing down my attraction to her since she showed up in my bedroom that night. It came out as hatred because I knew I didn't have a chance at trying to be something with her. It would never work. There was no point in letting her develop good feelings toward me."

"I guess that makes sense. Wow, you are such a sad man. You could have prevented all of this if you had just done it healthily!" Ayre looked at the mirror, and her face softened. Freya was tucked into bed and sleeping soundly. Ayre grabbed the bottom of the silk curtain covering one of the windows and yanked down on it. She then tossed it over the mirror and shook her head. "You can't peep on her any longer. Yes, we need to know more about the Mirror Realm, but we can't do it like this."

I shrugged my shoulders. "I was trying to figure out a way to get her back."

"You won't do that by staring at her." Ayre crossed her arms over her chest.

"No, but maybe I could learn something about her, to help me persuade her to come back to us," I said, dejectedly.

"Then she finds out you were spying on her?" Ayre let out a huff of air. "This is not going to go over well, I hope you know that."

CHAPTER EIGHTEEN

FREYA

I paced around the set of rooms that had been assigned to me. There was soft rose gold wallpaper from floor to ceiling. The carpet was plush ivory, and my feet literally sank down into it. I didn't even feel like it was appropriate for my shoes to even touch the rich material, so I set them on the seté in the corner of the room, by the bookcase full of books in other languages. I had tried to read one in my boredom, but couldn't understand anything on the page. All the letters and symbols floated around on the pages.

I had been so thankful I had packed some clothes until I realized there was a massive closet on the other side of the bathtub, stocked full of the most beautiful dresses I had ever seen. I ran my fingers over the materials gingerly, scared that the oils on my hands would mess them up.

"Those are for you." Cal's voice had me jumping out of my skin.

I placed my hand over my heart and glared daggers at him. "What if I was naked?" I panted.

"I guess that is the risk I was willing to take." He tried his hardest not to smile, but it only made his eyebrow quirk up in amusement.

"How charming." I crossed my arms over my chest, watching as his eyes tracked the progress of my t-shirt riding up on my stomach. His tongue flicked out and wet his bottom lip, sensually.

My lips parted slightly, and I couldn't help, but wonder what it would be like to kiss him. I blinked hard at my treacherous thoughts. I barely knew the man!

Get it together.

"I came by to see if you wanted to tour the kingdom." Cal's fingers fidgeted in front of him, and I wasn't sure if it was because of his nerves or it is an old habit.

"Really?" I asked, surprised.

"Yes, and as much as I praise what you have on, you will get more stares and attention then I want."

He bit his bottom lip and closed his eyes like I was going to change right then and there.

"That's possessive much, don't you think?" I raised my eyebrows at him.

He sputtered. "No, that is not why I said that. You can wear whatever it is you desire, I just figured that you might want to fly under the radar!" He sounded panicked, and I almost felt sorry for him.

I considered his words, realizing that he hadn't meant any harm. "Okay, go on then, I will be out in a few moments."

I pulled a red velvet number from the closet and laid on the chair next to the tub before I shucked my clothes and slid the impressive number up and over my body. It fit snugly against my skin, almost like it had been crafted just for me. I had growing suspicions that magic had a lot to do with it. Under all the gowns were slippers, they looked like something out of a fairy tale. I snickered and donned my converse. I felt guilty walking over the carpet in them, but I would figure something out to clean the beautiful flooring, if necessary.

When I pulled the double doors open, Cal was leaning against the door with a knife out, tossing it in the air. He looked up and grinned at me shyly before sheathing the weapon under his tunic against his side. His tunic was a dark gray today and was a little shorter than the one he had worn the day before, but where the one previously had been sleeveless, he had long sleeves today. His leggings matched, but they didn't seem to be as tight. He looked nicer, more formal. I imagined it had to do with our trip outside the castle walls. He was a prince, after all.

He put his palm on the small of my back and led me out of the confinements of the cinderblock walls.

"What is it like where you are from in the Earth Realm?" Cal looked down at me with twinkling, curious eyes.

"Dirty and humid." I tried to keep it light, but there was an underlying amount of disdain for the place I had come from. I had always been a southern girl, but the heat and mash of seasons all in one, made me feel a particular type of way.

"Sounds... Nice." His voice had a hint of amusement to it, but not much. Ugh, how could a person reply to that?

"Its full of life, and love and culture. But at the same time a lot of violence and poverty." I shrugged my shoulders trying to give him a better look into New Orleans. Though it hadn't been my home for long, I considered it my house more than I did the foster system.

"There isn't much of that here," he said as we passed some food carts. My stomach growled as the smells surrounded me. "There is a lot of magic, and that makes up for what people don't have. If they can't work, the magic can do some of it for them. If they are lazy, their magic will only do so much. Magic here is a great thing, but it has its limitations."

I could see that, but then again I wasn't sure how magic worked and had almost next to no training. I nodded my head, unsure of what else I could say. I felt ignorant and didn't want to admit it.

"Magic isn't a big part of the Earth Realm, is it?" We took a slight turn and ended up in a garden. The flowers growing well over my head.

I shook my head, not sure what to say. "I'm not really sure."

"I would imagine it's hidden from the humans, right?" He asked.

"Yes, definitely, I just don't know much about the witches on earth." He scrunched his face up as I spoke.

"How wouldn't you know?" He stopped and pulled me closer to him.

"I just found out I am a witch." I shrugged one of my shoulders up, taking a step away from him, looking at the roses dipping above our faces.

"How is that possible? Didn't you have magic as a child?" Cal frowned at me.

"No, I didn't have a magi." I touched mine tenderly.

"What is a magi?" He chuckled.

"Um, don't all witches have magis?"

He shook his head, then chuckled. It was a deep timber and had butterflies igniting in my stomach. "No, I have never heard of such a thing. Maybe my sister does, she is more interested in the human world than I ever was. But I have found a new interest in it." He winked at me.

I touched the soft petals on the rose above me and watched in wonder as it bloomed before my eyes. It's beautiful scent floated around my face and felt like a soft mist. I was sure it was the pollen falling out of it, and when I wiped my face, my hand came back with a powdery film on it.

"This was my mother's garden, I come here a lot when I need to think." He pushed through some overgrown weeds and brought me to a concrete bench. I hadn't expected us to be alone this whole time. I had thought we would be actually touring the kingdom.

He must have noticed my facial expression and chucked again. "Don't worry, we are just passing through. I wanted to bring you to my secret exit. There is no reason in us causing a hoopla in the village square."

He did have a point. Cal patted the seat beside him, and I brushed my dress underneath myself before sitting. My converse poked out from beneath the skirts of my dress, and Cal's eyebrows traveled up his forehead in surprise.

"Out of all the beautiful slippers in your closet, you chose some raggedy tennis shoes." He scoffed like a prince would.

I mocked being offended. "I had to wear these."

He raised an eyebrow. "Oh, why is that?" He leaned back slightly so he could take me all in.

"I can't run away from you in heels." I couldn't help the giggles that flew from my mouth at his shocked expression.

"You are one of a kind, Freya." He didn't laugh, but I could see the amusement in his eyes and in the twitch of his lips.

"So I have been told."

"I like that about you." He shook his head. "You seem very rebellious and headstrong."

"That's not the first time I have heard that either." I couldn't help, but keep laughing. The prince didn't know what to do with women like me. He was probably used to zombie-fied princesses that obeyed every command. I was no such lady. The giggling stopped, and I couldn't help the frown that spread across my face.

"What is it?" He stood up from the bench and picked a small rose, that hadn't grown to be as big as it's neighboring plants.

"I don't seem to fit in anywhere I go," I said a matter of fact.

"Why do you say that?" He gave me the little flower, and I tucked it into my hair, wanting to keep it forever.

"I was an orphan, and I didn't belong in any of the homes I was thrown into, I didn't belong in The Master's Coven, and I don't belong here. Is there anywhere I will ever belong?" I didn't know why I was putting my feelings out in the open, but there were so many thoughts rushing through my mind that I couldn't seem to keep them to myself.

"That must have been a tough childhood, I guess that makes sense since Sariah has been here since I was a baby and I don't know what happened to her husband, though he was supposed to be banished with her. He never came through with her." His words weren't quite registering in my mind, and I wondered if I had heard him correctly. I was about to ask when I noticed the grim look on his handsome face.

"No more serious talk, I'm sure that we will have more than enough time to do that later. Don't you have a kingdom to show me?" I pouted then smiled at him.

He flashed me his teeth in a breathtaking grin and pulled something from behind his back. "Yes, but we have to change. You will never experience this realm the way you are meant to if we are bombarded by fans the entire time."

He handed the bundle of fabric to me before materializing more bundles and shoes. He showed me behind a large bush of what looked to be cattails and ushered for me to change quickly. I let the red dress slip from my body before I pulled on the plain, robins egg blue dress. It had a few decorative buttons down the front and large pockets. It also hid my comfortable shoes, it was perfect. I draped the beautiful red velvet dress over my arm and came out from behind the cattails swishing in the wind. Cal was leaning against a dark violet tree with his dagger out again. I didn't know what he was working on, but he quickly sheathed it when he saw me.

His blond hair was covered with a leather brimmed hat, and he wore a thin white button down with leather pants. There were many daggers and what looked to be a whip strapped to his thighs. In these clothes, I could see his toned body better, and my entire being became fully aware of just how close I was to him. He was simply gorgeous. There was no other way to describe him. His face lit up when his eyes traveled my body, but I wasn't sure why. The material of the dress didn't precisely accentuate my curves or anything. I looked like any ole plain Jane. I twirled around for extra finesse. His lips curved up in an amused smile before he took my hand and placed it in the crook of his elbow.

"How gentlemanly." I looked up at him from beneath my lashes and grinned.

"I try, if my mother were still alive and knew that I wasn't one, she would have had my head! I'm sure she's relieved on the other side, knowing that her son finally stopped being a cad." Cal winked at me.

I didn't say anything as he brought us through a

small passageway in the bushes. There was a tiny door, and I raised my eyebrows at Cal in question. There was no way we were going to fit.

"Don't look at me like that, you act as if you haven't ever used magic before." Cal held up his hand, and something floated right above it. It twisted and turned in his palm, growing in size. It was an iridescent blue mist that I could almost see through. He tossed it at me and upon instinct, I went to catch it. But instead of landing in my hands, it exploded upon impact and sparkles rained down on me as I began to shrink, eventually becoming the size of Wyna. Cal was next, and his transformation was much faster. He pulled the key out of his pocket and went up to the little door. Well, now it was huge compared to us.

He unlocked the door quickly and pushed it open like he had done it countless times. He put his finger over his lips, while he yanked me through the opening. I had almost forgotten about my magi when it started to vibrate against my wrist. I felt uncertainty in the pit of my stomach and resisted his pull, yanking him back into the shadows with me.

He gave me a puzzled look, and I shook my head at him, just as a horse-drawn carriage zoomed by us. The large wheels rolling over the spot that Cal had just been standing on. His eyes got big, and he looked out, both ways before pulling me from the doorway. He frowned at me but didn't say anything. I kept my mouth closed, scared of why he had wanted me to be quiet in the first place.

We ran across the dirt road quickly before he pulled me against the trunk of a massive tree and let his magic soar my way once more. I was breathing hard by the time I was my average height, or at least I hoped I was. I patted down my body, making sure everything was the same, or what I thought to be the same. I smiled sheepishly at Cal when he gave me a funny look.

"How did you know that cart was coming?" Cal became serious quickly.

"I don't know, my magi warned me I guess." I held up my wrist to show him the beautiful jewelry there.

He picked my hand up in his and observed it carefully. "We are so much alike, yet so different. I wish I could visit your earth realm."

"Maybe one day we will both go back."

My words stunned Cal. "You mean you were actually serious?"

I shrugged my shoulders. "Why not? There is

nothing back there for me. Yes, I made a few friends, but fate brought me here for whatever reason."

He pulled me away from the shade of the tree, and I realized that we were in a field in the back of the castle. Standing not even 6 feet away from me was a massive mare. Her coat was a shining black wonder and the horn protruding from her forehead was just as magnificent. Cal gave me a toothy grin and made his way toward her. I stayed planted right where I was. The last thing I needed was to frighten a unicorn and get impaled. She sniffed Cal's fingers before eyeing me suspiciously.

"This is Eclipse. She's gentle, a little weary, but very gentle. I bring her to visit the children, so she's perfect for your first time." He ran his hand down the length of her mane, and his eyes softened. At that moment I wished I was an artist with the contrast between them. His light hair and her dark shiny coat. My fingers itched for my long forgotten iPhone back at the castle that was probably dead. Cal picked up his hat and readjusted it, flashing me a grin while he did so.

When I finally made my way toward them, I didn't touch the proud horse, too afraid for my life, but after a little coaxing, the mare had her snout in my hair and was trying to knock me over. The animal had a sense of humor, that was for sure. Cal pulled a brush out of thin air and started to work it down the glorious animal's body. After a few moments of that, he put the brush back where it came from. Then he had a carrot for her. She greedily ate it up.

"How do you do that? Are you creating things with your magic?" Pointing to where the carrot had disappeared to.

He frowned at me and became thoughtful. "No, it doesn't work like that. Some witches have magic like that, but not mine." He wrinkled his eyebrows. "You haven't had many lessons on being a witch, have you?"

I wanted to tell him yes, that I was more experienced, that I wasn't some ignorant woman that had landed herself in a foreign land, but all I could do was shrug and look to the soft bluegrass.

"There is nothing to be ashamed about. It's not your fault that you know nothing about being a witch." He held his hand out to me, and I took it hesitantly, unsure with the growing feelings I was having for him so soon. He was just so kind. "There will be plenty of time for you to go to classes, and learn about your own magic. But right now, I want to get to know you. I'm not worried about your knowledge of magic."

I couldn't help the smile that pulled at my lips, and I took his hand in mine. It was warm and rough like he spent many hours working with his hands.

"What do you do for fun?" I wanted to ask why his hands were so rough, but I kept it light instead.

"I like archery, and I spent a lot of my time training with the battalion."

"Why would a prince do that?" I raised my eyebrows in question as we made our way away from Ellipse and the field, I could see rising smoke in the distance and imagined we were getting close to the village surrounding the castle.

"Why wouldn't a prince? A good leader doesn't expect his followers to do all the work for him. A good leader is out there doing most of the work with them. I have to set an example for my men, no one is too good to fight for their country." His answer had me, and I hadn't realized I had been silent for quite some time until we came upon the first little home. Two children were playing out front, yelling and screaming. A woman watched from the window as she hung their laundry to dry.

"Why doesn't she use magic to dry her clothes?" I asked.

"Remember how I said some people have different types of magic?" Then I remembered what he had said about wanting time with me and not being an educator. I felt my face start to flame. Embarrassment flooded my entire being.

I nodded.

"She might not have an affinity with the elements." It made sense, and I decided to keep my questions to myself for the rest of the evening.

CHAPTER NINETEEN

I watched as the feminine looking Cal guided Freya to her rooms, she closed the door behind her with a soft click and sunk to the floor, happily. She looked intoxicated. I felt sick to my stomach. I had had a growing fixation with her and treated it all wrong, now here I was trying to play catch up in another realm.

I was stupid.

Ayre threw the doors to the study open and took one look at what I was doing and made the curtain fly back over the mirror with the flick of her wrist. "You shouldn't be here again."

I rolled my eyes at her.

"What would she do if she knew? First, you sneak into her room to get clothes and gaze upon her and now this?" She threw her hands in the air. "You are starting to resemble a lunatic."

"When I was gazing upon her, it was merely curiosity." I turned away from her.

"What is it now?" She stomped in front of me.

"I'm trying to figure out how to get her back!" I shouted.

"Why is that your job?" She yelled back at me.

"Because I drove her away," I said, softer.

She took a step closer to me. "That better be all it is, because from this point of view, you look like a peeping tom and it doesn't suit you, brother."

She slammed the door behind her, and I crumpled into my worn chair. I buried my face in my hands and knew that I wasn't getting anything done here, by staring at Freya through a magic glass. I didn't know how I was going to make it happen, but dammit, I wasn't going to stop until she was home.

My mother was the next one to confront me about my extracurricular activities. I knew better than to ignore my mother. The stormy look in her eye gave away too much.

"You have to let her stay there if that's where

she wants to be." My mother blocked my path in the hallway.

"How would you know that's what she wants to do?" I scowled down at her.

She rolled her eyes before she cocked her hip, annoyed. "Your father has the office spelled. There are too many witches in this compound to trust all of them. He has his protective measures that you don't need to worry with."

It sounded like Father. He liked his control. "Okay, so what do you want me to do?"

She bit the inside of her lip. "I want you to leave it alone. You can check on her for danger, you can watch to see if she changes her mind, but it isn't fair to her and her privacy to watch her every move."

I was offended. I could feel myself starting to get defensive, but I honed it in. "I don't watch her every move. There was a time she went to take a bath, I walked away. I'm genuinely surprised and offended that you would consider me in such a light." I could feel my magic starting to bubble under my skin. My magic warmed against my chest, and I patted my breast pocket gently. I didn't need any help fueling my magic today.

My mother's face fell, and tears welled up in her

eyes, guilt immediately taking over where her anger had been. "That's not what I was saying. I don't think you're creepy, but you are not honoring her privacy. Those conversations and moments with the prince are her own. You are taking that from her. Someday, if she comes back, and she wants to share those moments with you, that will be one thing. You are stealing these precious moments away from her. It's not fair to anyone."

She was right. I rocked back on my heels and nodded, nothing else needs to be said. She finally let me through, content with her mission. I walked around her quickly and pushed through the masses of people in the courtyard, no longer caring why they did what they did.

I shoved open the large doors at the end of the masses and was met with stagnant air and cigarette smoke. I ignored the humans making out at the other end of the alley and fled to the streets of the city I loved to loathe.

There were massive crowds everywhere, like a typical weekend. I wanted so badly to push them out of my town like it had been done just days prior. But as much as it was appealing, it made me sick to think of the dark magic that had been conjured in order to move all of those people. After what had happened to Sariah, my mother banned the teaching of dark magic in any context in the local Witchery Classes. Dark magic appealed to too many, even when it was barely spoken of. My mother preached that it wasn't supposed to be discussed at all.

We couldn't afford to lose any more witches to Sariah's crusade. Witches were coming up missing left and right, and we weren't sure if it was because Sariah was taking their power or they were willingly going to her to help her. I stumbled into a corner store and grabbed a bottled soda and Zapp's chips before going back out to the chaos of New Orleans.

Jazz surrounded me. The rich smells of Jambalaya and fried goods assaulted my nose. I inhaled deeply before crunching on my Voodoo chips. The spices always took me by surprise, even though it was my favorite flavor.

I took a sip from my coke and cringed. The flavors didn't go well together at all. People waved their hurricanes and daiquiris around as they made their way to Bourbon Street. Everyone seemed so carefree and happy today, not knowing that a dictator was about to cause more chaos than they could ever imagine. I shook my head at their ignorance. They did say ignorance is bliss.

I wondered, for a brief moment, what it would be like to be like them. No magic, far fewer problems. Like the fate of their city resting on one's shoulders. How glorious to drink their days and nights away, unknowing of what was to come.

My magi warmed up against my chest reminding me, that as much as this was my city,

I didn't belong here. I tossed my soda into the garbage and made my way toward the building that was steadily growing in the business district. I whistled at one of the taxis waiting on the side of the street and let him speed us to where

I needed to be. I would have transported myself there, but I had no idea what was waiting for me. Sariah was probably five steps ahead of me, if not more. I needed my strength if

I was going to go head to head with her, not that I wanted to. I threw a bunch of bills at the driver and hopped out. I had no idea what The human world saw before me, but what I was looking at was monstrous. I swallowed hard and popped my knuckles preparing myself for what was about to go down. The building was slowly stitching its self back together. It was possibly the crudest structure I had ever seen. Vines filled every crack and crevice. I hadn't learned much about Sariah, but I was almost sure she didn't have an affinity for earth magic.

Some witches were able to master many forms, especially the High Priestess.. but my mother hadn't mentioned anything of this magnitude. A building of this caliber took more power than one woman could muster alone. The front doors slammed open, and a short man with ebony skin walked down the steps.

"Mr. Masters, we have been expecting you," his voice choked out.

"Mr. Masters is my father, my name is Sterling. "I replied, cooly, even though my hands were sweating.

"We have formalities around here, young witch." He shook his head and pointed toward the doors. "This way, we shan't keep our High Priestess waiting."

It took us no time to get to the top of the growing building. From the inside, you couldn't even tell it was a building. Vines and flowers had overgrown on the walls and floors like a thick carpet.

Dread and unease filled my chest. My breathing felt constricted. The little man walked quicker than what I thought possible, and it was almost exhausting trying to keep up.

We walked up the stairs at an ungodly pace, I bent over wondering how I had gotten so out of shape. I considered myself healthy. I considered myself fit. I worked out and trained regularly with different types of weapons.

Why couldn't I keep up with the little man?

The man turned back to me and checked his tongue. "You are keeping our mistress waiting."

"That trek was tiring, for whatever reason." I panted.

He let out an exasperated found and continued on, but right before we made it to Sariah, I had an idol feeling that my magi needed to stay hidden. I let out a curse and tripped. The small man tapped his foot, irritated.

I grumbled, loudly while bending over. "I just need to tie these damned shoes."

He put his hands on his hips in a sassy manner. "Very well." When he turned away from me, I shoved my magi, that now was the size of a dime, under the sole of one of my shoes and quickly retied them.

"Let's get this show on the road!" I swung my fist in a mock jubilant swing.

He scurried forward and pushed open a door that had black roses covering it.

How fitting.

As we entered the room, I realized that the walls were covered in the same dark flowers and that was when I noticed Sariah standing against a huge cut out in the wall. Even with the opening, the room was still morbidly dark.

When Sariah turned around, I was taken back with just how much Freya resembled her. She didn't look a day over 26. Her red hair fell in heavy curls down her back. Her lips were painted a deep burgundy, and her curves were barely concealed in a tight green dress. The front dipped low, and her cleavage was pressed snuggly at the deep V there. I averted my eyes, suddenly feeling uncomfortable. "Really, sterling? I thought you would have preferred this." Sariah purred as she spun around provocatively.

"I don't know why you would think such a thing," I muttered.

"Word on the streets travels quickly, you are the womanizer of these parts, are you not?" She crossed her arms, causing her cleavage to spill forward even more.

"That may be so, but it has been some time." I

cleared my throat. "Cut the theatrics, you aren't here to seduce your old friend's son."

"You are correct." She said as she turned back to the gaping hole in the wall. "You wish to get my daughter back, too."

I folded my arms across my chest and didn't say anything.

"I am not stupid, I know I am not the only one that watches her." She turned back to me and materialized a new dress on her body. "I know she is fond of you. She sacrificed herself for your life. How touching." She ran her hands down the front of her new dress. I preferred this one more. It had a high neckline, and the bottom of it sat right above her knees.

"I was lucky. Nothing is going on between us." I shrugged my shoulders indifferently.

"Hm," She walked away from the broken up wall, toward a chair in the middle of the room. Then I realized it was a throne made out of roots. "That Cal is quite the character, don't you agree?" A picture of Cal and Freya holding hands appeared in my mind. I felt my hands clenching in response, playing right into her game. "For someone that hasn't been watching her, you sure react rather jealous."

"What do you want from me?" I was done playing her game.

"I want your help." She flicked her wrist forward, and a mirror floated from the opposite side of the room. It was identical to the one she had pulled Freya into. Its dark frame mocking me.

She moved her hands in front of the glass, and an image appeared on it. Freya running through a field full of flowers, Cal close on her heels. She let out a shriek as he got closer. It hadn't been that long since I had watched them interacting. How much time had they spent together for her to be this comfortable already?

I could have punched the glass when he finally caught up to her and threw her down to the soft looking field. The mirror flew away from me before I got the chance. "Ah, ah, ah! None of that. We need this mirror if we are going to get her back."

I pressed my palms into my eyes and groaned. "How is this possible?"

"Let me tell you a story." Roots sprung from the floor and created a seat beneath me. The amount of power in the room unnerved me. "I knew the magic I was messing with was tricky business. I had always known what dark magic did. I watched it destroy my father. I always said I would never do it.

I would never jeopardize my children and our standing in the coven. Do you think I planned for my son to die? Do you think I planned to go so mad that I tried to bring him back and lost my other child in the process?" She closed her dark purple eyes. "I didn't plan on being banished, but when I was, I took the necessary precautions to protect myself in case I got out. When I knew Freya was back, and I could get out, I did my plotting, and then I made the necessary arrangements to get her back."

I nodded my head processing what she was saying. "So, what do you need me for?"

"I never in my wildest dreams imagined that she wouldn't want to come back." She shook her head like she was disappointed in herself. "You are a means to an end."

How lovely.

CHAPTER TWENTY

Cal stared at me across the dinner table and lifted his water goblet in the solute.

Armia was pouting. "Ugh!" She grumbled as she shoveled food into her mouth. "I thought I was going to get a friend."

I was just about to say something when she continued on. "Cal, how many lovers do you need?" I spewed my water onto the table in a very unlady-like fashion. I then went on a downward spiral of not being able to stop coughing.

Armia just smiled sweetly and pretended like she hadn't just dumped out her brother's dirty secrets. Cal was now glaring at her and sending me sympathetic looks. I didn't mind. I knew what Armia was trying to do. I had met many girls like her in the many foster homes I had frequented. She was trying to be slick and drive a wedge between us so she could get more girl time. I didn't mind her wanting to spend more time with me. What I did mind were the games. Neither I or her brother deserved that.

I chose to ignore them both for the rest of the dinner. There was no point in getting in the middle of sibling rivalry. Wyna sat across from me and a woman I hadn't met yet perched on the other side of me. On the other side of me sat Armia. Wyna gave me a nervous glance before finishing up her meal. We hadn't had much time to talk or anything because of how much Cal whisked me away but at Armia's admission. I knew I needed a break from him.

I wasn't jealous or upset about what his sister revealed. I was okay with it and knew he needed to explore his options. He was, after all, the next in line for the throne. Many women would have been dying over the chance I had, but as I sat there and thought on it, I lost my appetite.

Cal and Armia were still bickering, and the woman beside me had stopped eating, as well. There were others dining in the room with us, but their faces all blurred together as I pushed away from the table.

"I think I'm going to retire for the night. Dinner was delicious." Cal opened his mouth, but I was already walking away.

Walking around the castle was like second nature now. I knew just about every room, though I hadn't been inside of the rooms. Cal had made sure I had the royal tour. He wanted to make sure I felt comfortable in my new home, but I secretly wondered if he had wanted me to know where his bedrooms were.

Once I was back in my room, I slid to the floor and spotted my long forgotten backpack under the chair beside me. I pulled it to me and yanked out all the contents. I dragged my clothes to my face and inhaled the scent of home. Homesickness hit me full force. I hadn't experienced it at all since arriving here. It was a foreign feeling. I conjured up the picture of Ayre in my mind and both of her parents.

I thought about how great they had been until; eventually, my mind dragged me to Sterling. I squeezed my eyes closed, not ready to relive how nasty he had been. I still wanted to kick him in his family jewels, but there had been a look of remorse when he saw me with my mother in the mirror. As if, deep down, he was a good person.

I shook my head.

Yeah, right.

THE NEXT DAY I donned clothes from back home, not understanding the deep ache in my chest. I pulled my backpack to me and seemed to hold on for dear life. I didn't think homesickness would attack me, especially after weeks had gone by. When someone knocked on the door, I ignored it. I wasn't in the mood to entertain. I felt like that was all I was. I cuddled the backpack closer to my chest and pulled the covers over my face. The knocking became more persistent until finally, the person went away. I had my suspicions it was Cal. I felt somewhat bad for ignoring him. I didn't want him to think it was because I was jealous or mad or even possessive. I just needed time to process my new feelings.

I must have dozed off because when I woke up someone was pounding on the door. My heart rate picked up, and my palms got sweaty. I stretched before I launched myself from the bed and yanked the door open.

Armia stood there shocked with her fist poised to knock. Her eyes grew wide, and her smile turned awkward. "Oh, hello."

I raised my eyebrows at her. "Hi, what's up?"

"Have you seen my brother?" She gave me a funny look, peering around me into my bedroom.

I frowned at her as she pushed past me and pulled the covers up, searching.

"No, why? Is something wrong?" I asked.

"You have spent the majority of your time here with him. No one saw you both leave the castle, so I assumed..." She trailed off, patting my hair.

I made a confused face and pushed her from my bedroom. She narrowed her eyes at me. I shouldered my backpack and closed the doors behind me.

"Are you sure my brother isn't in there?"She asked again as we walked away from my room.

I stopped. "Do you want to go look? What do you think you'll find?" She rolled her eyes. "I do not want to see my brother naked."

Blood flushed my face, and I shook my head.

I let out a sigh, no wonder she had made a comment about my hair. "After your comments, last night, do you really think I would just jump into bed with him?"

She shrugged her shoulders, causing her sleeves to fall on her small frame. She pushed them back up. "I've heard lover's quarrels can make you want them more."

"Well, I don't want him more. I have just been homesick." We passed a few guards, and they gawked at my clothes.

"So, you're ignoring my brother?"Armia paused and looked me in the eyes.

"No, I was taking a nap. You are certainly inquisitive this morning."

Her face went serious. "It's the afternoon. "

Of course, it was...

THE GAWKING HADN'T STOPPED with the guards, it had followed us out to the common folk. I didn't know why I was surprised, in almost all the time spent here, I had worn clothes of royalty unless Sterling snuck us out of the castle.

Armia ignored it, like everything about the situation at hand, Like my entire existence in this realm wasn't a huge thing. We passed a food cart, and Armia grabbed some fruit for us before paying the merchant heavily. She tossed a green orb my way and took a bite out of the thick shining skin of her wild-looking fruit.

Juice dripped down her chin, and she reached up and wiped it on the edge of her silk sleeve. My mouth fell open. There was no way she would be able to get that out of the fabric.

Wait... Magic.

We continued walking through the square until we heard a commotion up ahead. I dropped my fruit to the ground and watched out the corner of my eye as it rolled away. Armia looked behind us for her guards before she pulled her skirts up in her hands and took off running. She was a quick little thing, that was for sure.

I kept up easily, proud of myself for not wearing their constrictive clothing. My magi warmed against my wrist, reminding me of its presence.

My converse slapped the light purple dirt as I tried to keep up with her quick pace. She didn't look back as she continued forward. Finally, she stopped and didn't look out of breath at all, me on the other hand? I had broken out in a full on sweat and was resting my hands on my knees trying my hardest to breathe. Shouting was the only reason I looked up. There was a crowd, at What I assumed to be, the border.

Armia's hands were flailing around wildly, and I didn't notice the men staring me down on the other side until Armia turned back to me with a scowl.

Then I noticed them. The men were from the neighboring Kingdom, the Elves.

"You know it is protocol to inform all kingdoms of an outsider's entrance outside of the barren lands. How is this even possible?" The elf in front shouted in Armia's Face. I didn't know how she was standing there so calmly, I would have lost it.

In fact, my blood was starting to boil watching the exchange. I crossed my arms across my chest and narrowed my eyes at him. His blue-black hair was straight and long down his back, and a gold circlet was perched on his forehead. I guessed that meant he was royalty.

His eyes flicked from me, back to Armia. "Armia," He began. I watched as her shoulders relaxed, and she leaned toward him. "My father wants her."

She barked out a laugh as the elves started to close in around us and our measly few.

"Your father can't have her." She turned slightly so I could see her stick her tongue out at him. "Queen Armia, make sure you don't forget it. My brother will hate your tongue if he hears how familiar we have become."

The Prince rolled his eyes dramatically before he removed his hand from the sword at his side. "I am not afraid of your brother, Armia." The corner of his mouth quipped up in amusement. "But that is not what I'm here about, stop with the games, already. She is to come with me under Royal Decree."

When Armia turned toward me, I knew something was wrong. Her face was bright red, and she wouldn't look me in the eye. She wrung her hands in front of her before she started twisting a ring on her thumb.

"Freya," I didn't hear anything else she said. My heart thundered in my chest and drowned out all the noise around me. My body felt like it was being stung by a million wasps. Static lit up in my fingers. Everything went white as something scratched against my back.

Then everything came crashing back to me. I gasped as the sounds assaulted me. I blinked my eyes and tried to focus. Every single guard was turned toward me and had their various weapons were drawn, ready for attack.

The Prince had Armia shoved behind him, and

she was staring at me in horror. I didn't understand what was happening until a hot breeze hit my back. I let out a shaky breath and turned around slowly. The first thing I noticed was the orb from my backpack that looked like a dragon egg was broken in half. Whatever had come out of it was leaving a massive shadow over me. I swallowed hard and let my gaze travel up.

There right above me was a bright red dragon. If it hadn't had its tongue lolling out the side of its mouth, I would have been pretty afraid. But he looked just like a puppy dog staring at me like that. When the guards started to make their way back toward me, the ferocious beast let out a breath of fire, transforming into a hulking monster. They immediately backed off. Armia peeked her head out from behind the Prince's back, her eyes were half as big as her face.

The dragon tucked his wings in and made his way to my side while I overheard Armia muttering, "This isn't possible. Dragons are extinct. My Father killed the last one himself."

The creature snorted like he understood what she was saying. He rolled his serpent eyes. The yellow glowed maliciously in the setting sun's rays.

The Prince cleared his throat, regaining his

composure. I turned back to him, feeling more confident than I had before. "My father has ordered your presence in our Kingdom."

I pressed my lips together in irritation. "What if I say no?"

He sputtered. "No?" Then laughed.

I didn't think he was amusing either. My new friend must have agreed with me because I felt his warm snout press into my back. My backpack was in tatters around my feet. I kicked the material away from my feet before I dug my heels into the dirt, ready for a fight to ensue. I felt the dragon crouch low beside me, smoke rising up next to my face.

CHAPTER TWENTY-ONE

STERLING

I sat on the edge of my seat. It had been days since I had visited with Sariah. She had let me go willingly, but I knew it wasn't the last time I would hear from her. Especially after what was happening in The Mirror Realm right now. Ayre sat beside me, just as enthralled as I was. We hadn't moved. A dragon, a freakin' dragon. I leaned forward in my chair, anxiety twisting in my gut. I raked my fingers through my hair, glancing at Ayre out of the corner of my eyes. She had on a baggy sweatshirt that she hadn't changed out of in 3 days. She hadn't left my side or the mirror's since the damn dragon had burst from Freya's backpack.

Ayre had to spit her drink all over the room, shocked senseless. All she had been able to mutter was, "This can't be happening! We have to go see Madam Shriek. Immediately."

Madam shriek was the woman that owned the shop with Voodoo tokens and magis. We had stayed glued in the same spot as we were binge-watching something on Netflix. There was nothing we could change now.

We had watched entranced as the elves continued to push and Freya's fiery personality came to a peak. The dragon had nudged her again and then bowed low, perched ready for Freya to mount him. She thought on it for a second, assessing the situation before she jumped on his back. The beast pumped his wings twice and was gone in seconds. Freya's hair blending in with the dragon's scales. Fear lit up in her eyes before pure joy took over. She lifted her arms hesitantly before she tossed her head back and let out a holler. Then her hands flew up carelessly, and she laughed. When she opened her eyes, there was a weight lifted from her shoulders. Her hair whipped around her face as she looked out over The Mirror Realm.

Something had changed inside of me When I had watched her. It hadn't taken her long to make it back to the castle. The fairy was waiting for her when Freya's beast landed on the top. The Fairy had freaked out screaming about where they were going to house the monster. Freya had shrugged her shoulders before the dragon began to shrink, its gold eyes twinkled mischievously as it shrunk to the size of Freya's palm. He flew up and landed on Freya's shoulder, smirking in a dragon way. The little fairy rolled her eyes on.

The only thing that snapped me out of my thoughts of the past few days was the sound of Cal's voice over the mirror. It sounded like nails on a chalkboard, snapping me out of my thoughts.

"I can't believe you have a dragon." Cal laughed nervously. "What happened?"

She shrugged casually like it was no big deal. He had missed all the action and the bonding she had gone through in a short amount of time. "Where have you been?"

Cal looked around nervously as if he was going to evade the question altogether. "I had some business to attend to in a neighboring Kingdom ."

She nodded her head slowly, almost suspiciously. "Your sister filled you in?" she asked.

He nodded, then he flicked a dagger into the air before catching it effortlessly, the metal gleaming in the sunlight. He shoved his hands into his pockets before pulling something out. Freya looked surprised and shocked, but I couldn't tell what it was. She held it up in front of herself in wonder.

It was a small dragon carved out of wood, it resembled the one flying around them. She smiled before she pulled it to her chest affectionately., cradling it like a baby.

"Its what I've been working on since I first met you." He gave her a shy grin.

How was I supposed to compete with that?

"Wow, he's laying it on thick, isn't he?" Ayre said, scooping up popcorn before she threw it at me. I ignored the little fluff pellets as they rained down around me. I concentrated on the mirror and swallowed hard, it felt like glass was cutting its way down my esophagus.

"This is what you've been working on? What you've been so secretive about?"Freya asked Cal. His smiled beamed and I could have punched his lights out. I narrowed my eyes. Ayre snorted.

Freya pocketed the small figurine before she ran her fingers down the length of her dragon's snout. I still hadn't caught his name, and my curiosity was getting the best of me. I leaned back in my chair and stretched my legs out in front of me.

"How did you know to do a dragon?" I heard Freya ask.

Cal turned away from her, and I couldn't see his face, all I could hear was his reply, "You remind me of one."

Oh, you've got to be kidding me...

When Cal turned around, he was blushing. I barely noticed Freya rolling her eyes at him. She wasn't buying his bull. Atta girl.

I crossed my arms over my chest. Cal picked up on the change in her attitude, thank The Essence.

"So, do you know what caused this to happen?" Cal motioned his hands at the fire-breathing reptile.

If I were him, I would have been treading carefully. Freya held her hand out, and the massive thing rubbed against her like a feline. "I have no idea. I was going to go to the library and read up on them, but he's not allowed in there. I figured I could wait, at least until we figured out what is going on with the elves."

Cal dared to cringe, and I knew that the neighboring business he had been handling was the elves. "I think your magic awakened him."

She wrinkled her eyebrows. "Everything went white, I felt like my entire body was struck by lightning."

Cal bit his lip and Arye through a handful of popcorn at the glass. "Sounds like your body panicked and your magic felt life inside of the egg or the potential of life," he said.

She nodded her head and then looked down at her feet. "What did the elves want? Is that where Armia disappeared to? Or is everyone going to continue to lie to me and keep me in the dark?"

Cal cringed and scratched his head. Freya's hair had started to float around her face, her magic reacting with her emotions.

The dumbstruck man pulled his dagger from its sheath and fiddled with it, nervous. I stood up from my chair quickly, causing it to topple backward. I didn't know what I was going to do about it, but I was damned if I was just going to sit there and watch.

Freya didn't seem nervous at all, she flicked her floating hair from her face and turned away from him, uninterested in his nerves.

"Its been a very long time since we have had guests," he cleared his throat. "Peaceful guests from the Earth Realm."

"So, what do they want with me?" Her voice changed, and lightning lit up the sky. The dragon blew fire into the clouds before landing right next to Cal. He looked like he was going to jump out of his skin.

His Adam's apple bobbed before he took a step toward her. He placed his hands on either side of her face, and her hair immediately dropped to her back. I stepped closer to the mirror, dreading what was about to happen.

I could barely register Ayre's voice. I placed my hand on the cold glass. My body alights with my magic, my magi warm against my chest.

CHAPTER TWENTY-TWO

FREYA

My face flamed as Cal leaned in closer, every ounce of my being acutely aware of his presence.

He whispered against my neck, causing goose bumps to light up my body. I could hardly think of the speech I had prepared and practiced, for hours before. "I won't let them come for you, you must believe me, you aren't just some serving girl to me. You are royalty, everything about you. "

I swallowed against all the words bubbling up in my mouth as he got closer to my lips."Cal... You must understand..." I wet my lips with the tip of my tongue. His eyes following the innocent movement, that appeared sensual.

"Shh," He got closer, and there was only a tiny

gap between us. His breath warmed my parted mouth.

"I can't live here," Just as the words left my mouth, his lips replaced them. I pulled away quickly just as a deafening sound assaulted us. I blinked my eyes, and my jaw dropped open. Leaning against the castle wall was the mirror I had traveled through to get here.

But that wasn't what had me stunned, lying face down on the concrete was a man in a very familiar suit. As he picked his body up off of the cobblestones, dread coursed through my body. When he smiled at me, I knew I had to be dreaming. All Sterling Master's was capable of doing was sneering.

It was definitely a dream, or he had hit his head really hard on the ground. His pearly whites were aimed right at me. I blinked again, really trying to focus on what was going on. Then my eyes went back to the mirror. Staring back at me through the glass was Ayre. She had her nose pressed against it, looking like an adorable piggy. Her mouth was shaped in a perfect "O." Her sweatpants only added to her beauty, though I had never seen her dressed like that before. She started yelling, but I couldn't make sense of her words. She ran from the room and in all the time I had spent staring at her, I would have thought Sterling would have looked away from me. He hadn't. His smile was even more prominent.

Weird.

Cal had his daggers out, and guards were starting to mill around us. Their silver armor clanking with each step.

They pulled their swords out and pointed them at Sterling. His eyes twinkled with mischief. Of course, this would amuse him.

I knew that I was the only one that was going to stop this madness, but I didn't know if I wanted to. I figured this was good payback for the way he had treated me. His gorgeous smile wasn't going to make me falter. I tilted my chin up, ever slightly, giving him a motion that I was unaffected by his charms. His smile fell from his face. The guards approached him, ready to rip him up, but they hit an invisible wall and crumpled to the ground. Their armor sounding like nails on a chalkboard as it rubbed together.

Sterling pulled himself up, slowly, not taking his eyes from mine. I could briefly make out the sound of Cal shouting my name, but I ignored it. I didn't need anyone's saving or protection, I could do it on my own.

The only thing that jerked me from my thoughts was Cal grabbing my elbow. His grip was rough and too tight, I went to pull my arm back, but he was relentless. I glared at him, and my magic started to surge forward. My magi were scorching against my wrist.

"What are you doing?" Cal whispered in my ear.

"What are you doing?" At the sound of my voice, he released me. Sterling had his eyes narrowed at Cal, and I could see a storm brewing in them.

"We are in danger." Cal pointed to the jerk across from us. All amusement wiped clean from Sterling's face.

"I hate macho men for this very reason. No one thought to even ask the woman." I tasked and shook my head."How typical."

"Wait, you know this man?" Cal threw a dagger in the direction of Sterling, but it slowly melted mid-air and dripped onto the bodies of the fallen guards.

"Well, of course, I'm the only one not running around like a chicken with my head cut off," I said, dramatically.

Cal shook his head and made a confused face,

"What's a chicken?"

"How do you not know what a chicken is?" Sterling asked.

"Excuse me that I'm not up to date on the Earth Realm lingo."Cal bared his teeth at Sterling.

There was so much testosterone in the air, I couldn't breathe. Then Cal spoke up, and I could have died. "We were in the middle of something before we were so rudely interrupted." He smirked at Sterling like it was some kind of competition.

"Dude, nothing was going on, and you suck at reading body language. If a woman wants you, she'll be fluid in your arms, not stiff as a board. Sterling scoffed, and I was about to agree with him until something didn't make sense.

"How would you know what my body language was?" I narrowed my eyes at Sterling. He looked startled before he pulled himself together and gave me a cold stare. I wasn't buying it.

"I didn't have to see it before I came through. Anyone could notice your tension from a mile away." It was his turn to narrow his eyes.

Cal watched our exchanges with a scowl on his face. "You didn't want me to kiss you?"

Oh, boy.

"Cal," I started. His expression just got worse.

Great. "Maybe we should have this discussion in private."

He spread his hands full. "Might as well have it in front of our guest. He already knows more than what he's letting on."

I cleared my throat. "It's not that I didn't want to kiss you." I paused and rubbed my eyes. How had l managed to get myself in this situation? "I'm homesick."

At my admittance, Sterling looked more than satisfied. He crossed his arms over his chest, and my eyes followed the movement.

Cal pulled his top lip in between his teeth. "How long have you been thinking of going home?"

I let out a shaky breath, all of a sudden nervous. "Since the night before my dragon hatched."

"When my sister outed me for being woman crazed?" he asked.

I couldn't keep the giggle in that escaped my lips. "Yes and no. It was in that moment that I realized I didn't belong here either and that to solve my problems, I would have to fall them instead of taking the easy way out."

My eyes briefly left Cal's to land on Sterling's. He had a solemn expression on his face, and when he noticed me watching him, the corners of his mouth quirked up, almost in acceptance.

Cal nodded his head and began to speak, but I interrupted him."You deserve a Princess and someone that knows this Kingdom. Someone that knows this realm."

He chewed on his lip a minute more, before he looked at the mirror Sterling had come through. "It wouldn't be so bad to have an ally in the Earth Realm."

"Spoken like a true leader." Sterling spat.

That must have been the moment Sterling had enough of Cal. "Did you even have feelings for her?" I didn't know what the deal was and I definitely didn't understand the animosity.

Cal didn't answer, so Sterling, in his anger, flew across the small space separating them. Cal flicked his wrist and Sterling went soaring through the air, he landed hard on his back. Rainbow colored dust clouded around him. I had a small worry he had fallen on a fairy's home, but I knew they had a protected village so these things wouldn't happen by accident.

Sterling glared and dusted his suit off. The multi-colored dust started to float around him before it turned into a twister. Judging by Cal's terrified expression, they didn't have natural disasters here like they did in the Earth Realm.

I rolled my eyes, if this continued, it would go on all day. "Alright, children," I called.

Cal lowered his hands, and his lip went up in a sneer. I ignored him and continued, "I think its time I go home."

"I'll prepare my sister and Wyna." His voice lost its familiarity and was all business.

I nodded before he turned away. But then he pivoted back and grabbed my hand quickly. "Can I trust you will be safe with the Earth Dweller?"

I smiled at his concern. "Yes, he won't hurt me..." *Physically*, I finished in my head.

Cal squeezed my hand before he pulled away and headed toward the castle. We were in the pasture, and I was surprised we hadn't seen any of the unicorns.

Then I remembered my lizard friend, and it all made sense. He landed heavily infront of Sterling and let out a breath of smoke in his face. Sterling sputtered, and I let out a giggle. I still hadn't named the beast and felt terrible about it. I hadn't a clue of what to call him.

"Mischievous beasty," I snickered under my

breath. The overgrown lizard slowly blinked at me, clearly not amused.

"So, you're finally ready to come home?" I expected bitterness and resentment, but his voice was nothing of the sort. He seemed genuinely curious.

I thought for a second, taken back by his new attitude. He had never spoken to me so nicely. Apparently, this was a sterling from a different realm. He had to be. The Sterling from the Earth Realm didn't have a sincere bone in his body. Sterling waved his hand in front of the mirror in an arch gesture, and it shrunk.

He pocketed it and took a step closer to me.

"Yes, I'm ready to come home. Though I'm not entirely sure where home is." I made a move toward the castle, and my dragon friend took flight.

"It's at the compound with us." His voice matched his body language, and I wondered where the change had come from.

"I'm not so sure about that." My voice had taken a cold edge.

He stopped walking beside me. "Why not?"

I could have laughed. I almost did. "You have to be kidding me." I shook my head and continued on my way. I hoped he got lost.

He jogged to keep up with me." Okay, okay. I'm sorry."

I didn't stop walking. Each of my steps just continued to get more aggressive as I went. "And?"

"And I shouldn't have treated you like I did."He kept up with my long quick strides, but when he got to close my dragon swooped down to remind Sterling that he was still watching.

"Yeah," It was all I could say. I wanted to forgive him, but I also didn't know if this was some kind of ploy to get me to come back.

"Someday I'm going to make it up to you." He muttered as we entered the castle.

The guards eyed us suspiciously. It was one thing to have one Earth Dweller, but two? I patted the armor on one as we passed by, "Don't worry, we'll be out of your hair soon enough."

He didn't respond, just stared forward. Dragon followed on light feet behind us. I had an idea that Wyna would be in my room waiting for me. We hadn't had time to talk or visit since she had brought me here, but she was always off on royal assignments. I didn't know if it was true or if Cal had been trying to keep me to himself. It didn't matter now.

Sterling kept close to me, and Dragon kept extra

close to him. It made me want to giggle. I pushed the double doors open to my room and Wyna was perched on my bed.

Her smile got wider when her eyes landed on Sterling."Cal is such a liar. You are gorgeous." She completely ignored me and flew straight to jerk face. When she finally acknowledged me, I could have died. "And you didn't want to go back to this, why?"

"He may be gorgeous, but his personality sucks." Sorry, not sorry. His lips went from amused to grim very fast. I shrugged. All I spoke was the truth.

Wyna's eyes were huge. "I can't believe you would speak to him this way." She turned to Sterling. "You can leave her here and bring me home instead."

Well, then. "I'm going to miss you too, Wyna."

"Please, tell me that you will visit. " She flew back to me quickly and landed on my shoulder.

"Depending on how the mirror works, I would love to." I was being honest too.

I had come to love all the differences in this world compared to my home. I loved Cajun food, but there was nothing like the food here or the people.

Wyna pointed to the bed. Sitting at the foot was a leather backpack similar to the one dragon had destroyed. I smiled, it was a wonderful parting gift.

She clucked her tongue. "In case you ever need a reminder of your time here, just reach into your pack, and my magic will do the rest."

I wasn't at all surprised that Armia skipped out on seeing us off, though I was surprised that she missed how good looking Sterling was. Wyna made a comment about it before the thought even popped into my head. It made sense. She seemed like the type to like a good bit of eye candy, Wyna's words. Cal kissed my knuckles and let us be.

The mirror leaned up against the wall in my rooms, and my dragon had shrunk to size to be able to go through. Sterling pressed his palm against the glass, and the reflexion started to ripple, looking fluid. He poked his head through and then popped back out.

"I needed to make sure we were going to the right place." He gave me a sheepish grin. I couldn't return it, he was acting too sweet for my comfort.

"I think it would be fun to randomly pop in somewhere." I gave him a Cheshire grin and cocked my head to the side. "Dinner and a show."

He didn't even crack a smile. Ahh, the facade

was almost over with. "Come on now, we don't want any interruptions."

I stepped through the fluid material, and my body swayed. I felt myself tilt and the world went sideways. I recognized the library as the room went dark. Strong arms caught me, and I let myself fade peacefully into the water like substance I seemed to be caught in.

CHAPTER TWENTY-THREE

STERLING

I was almost a second too late. Freya's small frame collapsed into my arms. Her red locks fanned out around her face and almost touched the floor. Her eyelashes fluttered, but her eyes didn't open. Her thick eyelashes fell against the freckles under her eyes. Her dragon blinked slowly and licked his teeth, almost as a warning. Ayre rushed forward and waved her hands in front of the mirror, the water like substance turned to tar. My mother was the next one in the room.

"They will come for her. You must know that." My mother rushed forward and tried to take her from my hands. I pulled away, not keen on the idea of letting Freya go just yet. There was something comforting about being able to touch her. I didn't know why, but I enjoyed it. Her presence, where it had bothered me before, it now soothed me.

"There isn't much we can do about that," I brushed a few loose strands of her hair from her forehead and swallowed hard.

"She is the only one that can dethrone Sariah." Ayre paced back and forth in front of us.

"I know," I said.

My mother cocked an eyebrow. "Is there something you need to tell us?"

"I met with Sariah." I looked down at the look-alike in my arms and felt my stomach starting to hate me. Nausea was the best indicator of my nerves. "She told me that I was the only way to get Freya back."

My mother's eyes grew dark. "Is that so? How did she think you were to do that?" My mother pushed the doors open to the study and lead me to Freya's bedroom. She wasn't a big girl, but my arms were starting to fall asleep, and as much as I longed to hold her, I knew I couldn't wait for much longer.

"I don't know. I think her homesickness and my reacting was simply a coincidence, but honestly, I wouldn't put it past Sariah to have pulled some elaborate scheme out of a hat." When I entered Freya's bedroom, I was relieved with the fact that my father had been thoughtful and actually positive about the situation. He had been more proactive than I had and had either ordered her an entire bedroom set or had used magic. He loved to spend money, so I was sure he had done just that. I laid her down on the soft green bedding and smiled.

She looked like a picture perfect sleeping beauty, and I was confused as to why I hadn't seen it before. I had been so adamant on hating her that I hadn't realized her potential with magic or her beauty. I had poisoned my own mind with my bad thoughts. Her dragon cuddled up to her, and when I went to say something about it, his nostrils started to smoke. Ayre just stared at the monstrous beast in shock, her mouth hung open slightly.

"That thing is very interesting. Are you sure we should leave them alone?" My mother asked.

In response, the dragon shot out a bit of fire into the air, daring her to do something about it. My mother put her hands up in surrender, and we closed the doors. I leaned against the dark wood and peaked in the window to make sure I could still see her. Sariah would be making her appearance soon, this had no doubts about.

"What do you think Sariah will do?" Ayre asked us both. I didn't say anything for a moment, too wrapped up in my own thoughts to even think on hers.

My mother was the first one to speak, "She is very sneaky, but she loves the praise of her accomplishments. She will want to take credit for her daughter being back in the city, or rather just this realm."

"There is much to be discovered about the Mirror Realm," I said, quietly.

"If anyone knows anything about the Mirror Realm it will be Madam Shriek." My mother muttered.

"Why does it keep coming back to her? I see a cycle here that I don't like. First the dragon egg and now she knows the most about the Mirror Realm?" I said, incredulously.

"Would you rather speak to her or your father?" My mother crossed her arms over her chest, and her eyebrows pinched together in anger. "Your father didn't give her the dragon egg and isn't a seer. On top of that, it's probably still a good idea to at least bring him up to speed, to get his input on the situation."

I peeked through the window and watched as Freya rolled over and blinked her eyes open. "I'll let Freya decide that. She seems to have found father's soft side."

My mother's face relaxed a tad and her lips quirked up gently. "I think that's a good idea."

Ayre shoved me away from the door and rushed to her friend. She didn't have a care in the world as she held Freya close. Her eyes were squeezed shut as if Freya would disappear if she opened them. Like she had the best dream, and she couldn't dare to wake up from it. When they pulled apart, it was like they had never separated. Their friendship picked up right where it left off. Their faces lit up, and their hands went flying as they both quickly filled each other in on what had happened while Freya was away.

Freya's eyes flicked my way, and her face fell. I looked to the worn floor panels and walked away from them both. There was no use in trying to be a part of something I was not.

My mother caught up with me. "You can't expect her to be warm to you. In fact, you can't really expect anything from her. You messed up."

"So, what do I do?" I turned away from her and looked out to the compound.

"You take it day by day and make it right. She will never forget what you did or what you said, but you can try to earn her forgiveness." My mother's hand trailed down my arm, and she took my hand in hers. "You can be a wonderful person when you want to be. Start choosing that side of yourself and she'll see it. It might take a while, but she will." She squeezed my fingers before she left me there to ponder her words.

THE COMPOUND WAS QUIET, though that wasn't unusual for a weekend. Many of the witches that lived in New Orleans weren't from here. They had been drawn here by our essence, and many of the others were here for sanctuary, from their own people or past covens, for whatever reason. We didn't ask army questions. I was sure my father knew much more than he led on too. He had his ways, and his magic was much different than any other witch I met.

My father didn't have a Magi. He wore many ornate pieces of jewelry, and it threw everyone else off. Everyone in the coven figured one of the many rings he wore was his magi, but I had seen him remove every single item from his skin. It would have caused him pain like no other to remove a magi. Like Ayre had told Freya. My mother had changed the subject any time I had brought it up. Ayre laughed it off like I was speaking crazy. I probably was. I didn't speak about it to anyone else, but as I paced my room, I had this growing thought. I tried to push it from my mind. I pressed my palms into my eyes, groaning in frustration.

I was acting crazy. This was crazy, but I did it anyway and shoved my bedroom doors open. I held my fist up and attempted to knock. She had put up thick orange curtains, and I couldn't see into her room. I held my breath and took a step backward. Then the double doors swung open and there she was. Her hair was braided away from her face, and she was wearing pajamas. I went to smile but realized she was scowling, so I continued to take a step back again.

"Can I help you?" She crossed her arms over her chest, closing herself off.

"Uh," My mouth went dry. I had never had issues insulting her or being mean. "I just wanted to talk to you about the Mirror Realm, it seemed very different."

"Different is an understatement," she said, coldly.

"Look, I'm not the enemy here." I held my hands up in surrender. "I just want to talk."

She bit her bottom lip and let her shoulders fall. "Fine," she mumbled.

"It's mostly about my father," I said.

She narrowed her eyes at me. "I don't want to get in the middle of your family issues."

"It's not like that." I paused. "They don't use magis in the Mirror Realm, right?" I barely remembered hearing that in one of her conversations with Cal, but I needed to know.

"They don't have magis, no." She sat on the corner of her now empty bed. The dragon nowhere to be seen, but the balcony window was wide open. I wondered how much time we had before he returned. I figured my best bet was to stay close to an exit, just in case.

"My father doesn't have a magi either." I let it process for a moment. Her eyes got wide. "My mother told me to talk to him about the Mirror Realm."

She nibbled on her lip for a minute. Her eyebrows furrowed in thought. "Do you think he's from the Mirror Realm?"

"I'm not sure, but its suspicious. " I leaned against the wall and tried to keep my eyes off of her. A few strands of hair had escaped the knot on her head and were framing her face now. My fingers itched to brush the frays of hair behind her small ears.

"You don't have a good relationship with your dad, do you?" She pulled a pillow from the head of the bed and hugged it close to her chest.

I shook my head. "Not entirely."

She frowned. "I'm sorry, I wish I had known my father."

Guilt surged through my body. Here I was having stupid animosity with my father, and she had never met hers before. She probably would never get to know him. I wasn't sure who he was either.

"I wish I could help you know who he is, but that was before my time." I shoved my hands into my pockets. "Well, before the time I remember."

She nodded and sat back. "You've always lived in the compound?"

I looked away from her and looked out to the night. I could barely see the night stars, but they were there; just distant. "Yes, I've never left New Orleans. My mother is the High Priestess, so she leaves on business often, but we are always required to stay home. It's safer here."

Freya gave me a sympathetic look. "I'm sorry I've been cold, you have been nothing but nice to me since I got back..." She trailed off and closed her eyes. My mouth went dry, she was good. She was the kind of good I didn't deserve.

"There is absolutely nothing you need to apologize for. I don't deserve this small talk. My character was despicable. I don't know why I reacted to you that way." I scrubbed my hands down my face. "But I never plan on acting like that again. I am the one that is sorry."

A crash had me jerking my head toward the doorway where Ayre stood with her mouth agape. Two broken mugs were at her feet. The brown contents splattered on the doors and the bottoms of her light pink leggings. She waved her hand dismissively, and the pieces started to put themselves back together above the ground.

"Did he just apologize?" Ayre let the mugs do their thing as she came farther into the room. Her magic doing all the work for her as her mind processed what was happening.

I rolled my eyes. "The theatrics were cute when you were a toddler, but they're just plain annoying now."

She stuck her tongue out at me, and the softest of giggles had me whipping around. Freya had her hand over her mouth and the prettiest mischief twinkling in her eye.

Ayre let out an exasperated huff and rolled her eyes. "Fine, you two get cozy, I'll go and make some more hot chocolate." She cocked her hip and looked at me. "But when I get back you better be gone. Freya promised me a Harry Potter marathon, and she swears they're good. I don't need you around sucking all the fun."

"She secretly enjoys me spending time with you." I snickered.

"I don't believe you at all." She laughed.

I shrugged and was about to say something when she beat me to it, "How did you know they didn't use magis in the Mirror Realm?"

We were starting to get on better ground, I didn't want to destroy that by lying. "When we repaired the mirror, we were able to watch you."

Her face turned almost as bright as her hair. She stood up from the bed quickly, marching toward me. "You watched me?"

"Not entirely." I moved my weight from one foot to the other, afraid she was going to hit me again.

I wondered if I should wait it out and help her simmer down or flee.

"What is that supposed to mean?" Her hair was starting to lift from her shoulders.

"I was obsessed in the beginning. I had driven

you away. I was the reason for everything. All I could think about was fixing the situation. Being back in my parent's good graces." Her eyes softened as she looked up at me, but her hair continued to float." Then I saw you. You were brave and fearless and nothing I had played you out to be. At every single turn, you proved me wrong."

"And then what?" She took a step back.

"And then my mother and Ayre put it into perspective, and I stopped." I bit my lip. "After that, I only watched to protect you. Sariah started a new game, and I don't want to scare you, but I was afraid."

"Is that when you decided to come for me?" She twisted a strand of hair around her finger, and her Magi caught the light just right, sending thousands on red sparkles onto the wall.

"Not exactly." I dragged my hand across my brow. She lifted one of her strawberry blond eyebrows at me in question. "My emotions put me through the mirror. I couldn't stand to see him touch you." I took a hesitant step toward her. She was just within my reach. "You don't know me like I feel I know you."

I could have smacked myself. I sounded like such a creep. I closed my eyes and stepped away from her. She was too good for me anyhow. I fled the room and was just about to escape the compound when I heard Arye yell. "Ugh! You fun sucker!"

CHAPTER TWENTY-FOUR

FREYA

Harry Potter droned on in the background. Where it had been one of my favorites, I could hardly focus on it. All I kept thinking about was what Sterling had seen. What had I done while he had watched? It was consuming me.

Ayre's shoulder bumped mine and jostled me from my thoughts. "I really hate him sometimes." She sipped on her hot chocolate audibly. Mine sat untouched. It was too hot in Louisiana for that. "What did he say to you anyhow?"

"Did you know that Sterling watched me while I was there?" Her eyes grew to the size of saucers and answered my question. "And you and your mother stopped him?"

She paused the movie. By the looks of it, we were on the fourth one."We were worried about you there... " She trailed off and didn't continue.

"And?" I crossed my arms over my chest, agitation filled my voice.

"And what? He saw you getting cozy with Cal, that slimeball." I narrowed my eyes at her. By the sounds of it, she was team Sterling all the way. Not that it mattered, I tried to reason with myself. There were no teams.

"Cal is in another realm. You two realize that, right?" I asked, incredulously.

"A realm that you can easily get to, through a mirror." She raised her eyebrows at me. She had a point, but still.

"Well, if you were both peeping toms then you would know that he is a player and his own sister called him out." I quirked an eyebrow.

"I don't know, something was really strange about it all." She said. She narrowed her eyes at me.

"Whatever. He's gorgeous and a prince, what's suspicious about that?" I watched the windows at the balcony, worried my beasty had gotten himself into trouble.

"Oh my gosh, what's not suspicious about that?" She threw her hands up in the air.

"Nothing, never mind, forget I said anything," I mumbled.

Ayre's face softened. "Okay, I'm sorry, I shouldn't be arguing with you. I just got you back." She grabbed my hand in hers. "Tell me about it."

What was there to tell? She had already watched it all unfold before her, like a movie.

"Okay," I closed my eyes and imagined the sweet smell oo the air. The air I had come to love.

I imagined the fairies and the unicorns and all the things I would probably never experience again. After a few moments of silence, Ayre gasped. My eyes flew open. I expected my dragon to be back. She had her hand covering her mouth. "Is that what it's really like there?"

"What do you mean?" I asked, now worried.

"The smell in here, you're doing that, right?" My hands were open, palms down and fingers splayed out. There was the smallest amount of pink mist floating off of the tips of my fingers. It reminded me of the pollen from Cal's mother's garden. When it started to coat the hardwood floors, I knew that my magic was creating it. I had thought it was just an illusion, but when I touched it, the powder coated my fingers in a thick film.

"I've never seen anyone do that before." She

trailed off. Almost as if on cue, my dragon landed on the window's ledge. He had shrunk to the size of Wyna and blinked at me slowly, almost sizing me up.

Ayre gave me a worried glance. "What's his name?"

"I'm not sure yet, I don't think he would appreciate me trying to name him. I'm almost certain he already has a name, and I just need to figure it out." The dragon tolled his tongue out happily, and I knew I had answered correctly.

"So, what are you going to call him until you figure it out?" Ayre took a step closer to the red monster.

"Hmm, well," I paused and thought for a moment. "I always call him my beasty."

The animal in question snorted loudly and then rolled his eyes. He would probably find some way to tell me VERY soon if I kept it up.

"I don't think he likes that very much." Ayre covered her mouth as she giggled. "He won't hurt me, right?"

I shook my head, "Just don't provoke him. I'm sure he would have no problem showing his power." I turned to beasty as he was starting to grow bigger. "So, where did you go off to?"

He lazily walked back to the window and motioned with his head for me to come too. "What is it, boy?" He pressed his snout to my hand, and I was transported from the room. Everything I was seeing, it seemed as if I was gazing through a fish-bowl. Then I realized I was experiencing a memory through my dragon's eyes and I was in his shoes, so to speak.

My mother was looking out a gaping hole, in what looked to be, a dystopian tower, held together by vines and black roses. She rolled her eyes and paced. "She has been back in this realm for a few hours, and we have heard nothing?! You were supposed to guarantee that she would want to come back through the mirror I gave you!" She shouted at something, but from the dragon's view, I couldn't see. He moved slightly and flew to another rooftop, blending with the shadows.

"It wasn't me that saw her through the mirror. I was in the Eleven Kingdom and didn't think things would escalate so quickly." There was something about the voice. Something familiar that I couldn't place. Almost as if on cue, the dragon moved again to get a better look at the person Sariah was talking to. It was a mirror that matched the one that I had gone through, but her's was gold and not bronze.

"I told you to leave that stupid prince alone until everything had been finalized." Sariah moved slightly, and I got a glimpse of Armia in the mirror. It all made sense. She had a thing for the Elven Prince, and I didn't know why I hadn't seen through her facade sooner. She had been far too inviting. I swallowed hard, wondering if Wyna was in on it all also, I had come to really like her.

"The stupid fairy didn't listen to me and sent her off quickly," Armia said.

"Do you think she knows?" Sariah asked, worry taking over her flawless face.

"No, she doesn't suspect anything," Armia replied, giddy.

"Perfect. And the dragon?"

"I don't have any idea. They have been extinct for years, this shouldn't be possible, at all." Armia turned away from the mirror before she looked at Sariah solemnly. "I think it's her magic. I couldn't get a good read on her when we spoke or anything, but before the dragon burst forth, I felt power like I have never experienced. If he is her familiar their bond will continue to grow, and his magic will intertwine with hers. They will be unstoppable."

"How do we stop this bonding?" Sariah asked,

biting her lip. I caught myself doing the same thing and grimaced.

"You'll have to kill him first. With his magic aiding her, it will be harder for you to control her or get her on to our cause." Armia went to say something else, but my dragon was already flying away. If they got their hands on him, they wouldn't hesitate to take him out of the equation.

My dragon removed his snout from my skin, and I was brought back to the present. He looked down to the floors before he looked back up at me. Worry was shining brightly in his eyes.

Ayre just sat on the bed with her mouth hanging open. "Well, that was weird."

"What?"

"Oh, no big deal, your eyes just were open, staring blankly outside and they were the eyes of your dragon. Your human eyes were gone." Her voice sounded terrified, but I couldn't help but smile. I figured that was all apart of the bonding and we needed that to happen.

The dragon nodded as if he heard my thoughts. He nodded again to confirm my suspicions. I winked at him. This could be kind of cool. Scary, but cool.

"Soooo, what happened?" Ayre crossed her

arms over her chest and gave me a suspicious glance.

"Sariah is planning something with the Mirror Realm," I said.

"Maybe we should get my parents in for this one." She muttered before she fled from the room.

My dragon gave a sideways glance, wondering if this was a good idea. I nodded to him, trying to reassure him.

Ayre's parents were in the room rather quickly, but Sterling wasn't with them. A little bit of curiosity touched my mind, but I quickly pushed it away. I could almost hear the snicker of the dragon in my mind.

"Oh, hush you." I pointed at him and tried my hardest to give him a serious look.

"Interesting," Jonathan said from the doorway. "Looks like our new little witch has gained herself a familiar."

Camey looked at me surprised then looked at her husband. "I haven't heard that term used in a very long time."

"If a familiar is what I think it is, then I am pretty sure that is what her dragon is," Ayre said quickly.

"He is my familiar, but we haven't gone through the bond yet," I said.

Jonathan raised his eyebrows at my confidence. "What makes you think this?"

"Sariah told Queen Armia in the mirror earlier tonight." My voice sounded cold.

Camey looked at her daughter, then looked back at me. "But neither of you left the compound tonight. How would you know…" Her voice trailed off as she looked at the dragon resting on my bed with one eye open, lazily listening to the entire conversation.

"He left the compound a few hours ago to hunt or do whatever it is he does. He came back with knowledge instead." I said, pride shining from me.

Jonathan took a few timid steps toward the scaled monster. "I'm not going to hurt you, I just would like to confirm some theories."

"Theories? I hate the Mirror Realm witches." A voice boomed in my mind. I whipped my head up, and the dragon rolled his eyes at the slow approaching man.

My thoughts were a jumble, and I didn't know if I could even think a coherent thought back to him. I wrinkled my eyebrows and tried it out. The dragon's shoulders just slumped with each of my attempts.

"How do you know he's a Mirror Realm witch?" My thought must have gone through loud and clear because the beast winced and gave me an agitated glare.

"They are growing suspicious, you must learn to multitask, Earth Dweller."

I rolled my eyes and answered audibly. "Whatever, dragon. How old are you again? Also, you're an Earth Dweller too."

The dragon let out a breath of smoke and hopped from the bed. Jonathan scurried backward. It almost made me laugh. How interesting that a dragon would have a powerful witch scrambling around like this.

"I don't mean to interrupt, but from ancient dragon text, I have read that dragons are reincarnated," Jonathan said, making an attempt to get closer to my familiar.

"I would love to hear more about this text," Camey said, narrowing her eyes, almost suspiciously.

Jonathan was about to ignore her when my dragon friend had other ideas. He spit a quarter size amount of fire, and it hit Jonathan's shiny leather shoe. He jumped up and tried to put the flame out with his magic, at least that's what I thought he was doing with his wild flailing hands. "Okay, okay, you can put the flame out now." He grimaced in pain and kept stamping his foot; finally, my friend put the flame out with his saliva.

"I read about dragons in the Mirror Realm once." He paused.

Camey opened and closed her mouth like a gaping fish. "I always knew. I always knew that you had a major secret life that I wasn't a part of."

Ayre just looked plain uncomfortable and kept giving me a strange smile.

I interrupted, putting my hand up. "How about we wait for Sterling to have this conversation, Mirror Realm dweller?"

Jonathan's eyes flicked from me to the dragon, and he shook his head. "Dragons are brilliant creatures, and you are lucky he chose you to be his witch."

I frowned and looked at the creature perched on my bed. He just rested his head on his front legs and closed his eyes, choosing to ignore me. It was all the answer I needed.

"Anyway, when he got back, he pressed his nose against my skin, and I saw his memories."

Ayre interrupted my retelling of it then. "And her eyes mirrored his."

Jonathan nodded, and Camey leaned against the wall for support, she looked way out of her element. It reaffirmed to me that she wasn't ever meant to be the High Priestess. Since getting thrown into all of this mess, I kept coming back to her, wondering if it was just a mistake, that she was the one meant to rule. But as I looked at her, with confusion apparent on her face and dread filling her eyes, I knew that she had put on a brave face and done what she had to for her people. She had faked it till she made it, but she had done what she needed to. Now that she no longer held those powers, it was evident that she was losing her grip on the leadership role.

"Queen Armia was in the mirror. She is the Queen of one of the four kingdoms in the Mirror Realm. She has a budding relationship with a prince in the Elven kingdom, and I was romantically involved with her brother, Cal." I took a deep breath, trying not to look anyone in the eye. "I don't believe Cal is involved, but I am worried about him. He has no idea that Armia is working with Sariah, and I don't know how long they have been in cahoots."

"What did you see?" Jonathan grabbed his wife's hand, and his thumb rubbed circles on the inside of her wrist, reassuringly.

"She has another mirror, and she intended Armia to send me home through it, so I would technically be stuck with her as soon as I went through. I'm guessing that she didn't expect Sterling's emotions to bring me home. They don't want me to complete the bonding with my dragon." I closed my eyes and shook my head. "I don't know why, he came back before they were finished, but at least we have some idea of what we are up against."

Jonathan bit the inside of his lip. "I wish I knew what they were planning, but it was a good thing that your dragon came back as soon as he did. If they had spotted him, they could have taken him out." Jonathan looked to the beast on the bed, his eyes were still closed. "You probably already know this, but until you are fully bonded to Freya, you can't leave the compound. We can't risk you getting caught by them. You are a new dragon and not as healthy or as strong as you were in your previous life."

The dragon didn't open his eyes or even acknowledge Jonathan. I guess he wasn't a fan of the man. It didn't seem like many cared for him either.

"Vailen." The dragon's voice whispered quietly through my mind.

"His name is Vailen," I said, as I smiled.

It was Jonathan's turn to smile. "I see the bond is becoming stronger. This is good. We need to formulate a plan, but it is getting late, and I need to find Sterling." He pulled his wife off of the floor, and she smiled at me sleepily and laid her head on Jonathan's shoulder.

Ayre pushed Vailen out of the way and pulled my comforter around her shoulders. "I'm sleeping in here tonight. Goodnight world."

Vailen just rolled his eyes and pushed her off the bed with his thick tail.

CHAPTER TWENTY-FIVE

STERLING

The music thumped wildly around me, and I felt an odd sense of déjà vu. I knocked back a shot, knowing full well what it would do to me and I surveyed the floor. I hadn't felt the pull to come back, but I had come anyway. New faces littered the dance floor, but there was nothing that set them apart. The people were all the same. Same hair, same clothes, and the same drug hazy eyes and the sheeple mindset. Why had I allowed myself too enthralled by these people? What had pushed me to want to wrap myself in their embraces almost nightly? And the worst question of all, why was I back here, to begin with?

I didn't know the answers to the other questions, but the last one? I knew it All too well.

Freya.

I didn't understand why she was stuck in my thoughts still. She had given me proof time and time again about her character while she hadn't even realized that was what she was doing. Yes, she was special.

But was she really this special?

A brunette across the dance floor caught my eye. Her lavender eyes glittered mischievously. She smiled at me and motioned me to meet her. I hadn't seen her before, and when I got close to her, her exotic scent pulled me in. Then I realized, besides her eyes, what had drawn me to her. She wasn't like the others. She was wearing a pantsuit and was holding a glass of wine.

I nodded my head toward her glass. "I think you're in the wrong place."

"Perhaps, but it just got more interesting." I couldn't place her accent, though I wondered if it might be French.

I leaned against the wall, and her eyes watched my every movement. "I have to agree."

She took a sip out of her glass and looked away from me as she spoke. "I hope that I'm not asking the wrong person this, but I'm in search of the Master's Compound."

My back straightened on its own accord. "Who's asking?"

"I'm Shay DeVille, I'm from the coven in Paris." She looked away from me again.

"Really? What brings you here?" I said coolly, as I crossed my arms over my chest. My head was starting to spin, but I was trying to play it off. I should have known to stay away from the poison.

"I'm on the run from my past. I understand there is a slight turf war going on, but the essence calls to me here. More than anywhere else, even Paris." She tilted her wine glass and sloshed the drink around the rim.

I nodded my head. She wasn't the first and wouldn't be the last to come to us, for the same exact reasoning. "I'm Sterling Master, it's nice to meet you, Shay."

The walk back to the compound was comfortable and a first. I had never left a club slowly or with a woman I wasn't trying to get naked. Not that I didn't want to, I just didn't feel so rushed. I actually wanted to get to know her. It also didn't help that my magi was trying to burn off the effects of the alcohol I had consumed.

One thing I knew for sure, I couldn't keep my

eyes off of her, or the way her body filled out the pantsuit, and I hadn't thought of Freya once.

When we reached the compound, my father was waiting outside of the doors. He stared at Shay menacingly before he addressed me. "Where have you been?"

"I didn't realize I needed to put my every move by you." My tone and stance matching his.

"No, but something happened tonight." The anger on my father's face started to melt away to fatigue and worry.

Dread coated my insides. Freya.

I forgot about the woman beside me and sprung to action. I raced through the courtyard and up the stairs. I would never forgive myself if something happened again.

I ignored my father's shouting and pushed Freya's doors open. My worry and dread eased and turned into guilt. Laying at the foot of the bed was the dragon and on either side of him was Freya and my sister. He blinked his eyes open, and smoke started to curl up from his nostrils.

"Vailen will kill you." Freya's sleepy voice floated across the room. She didn't open her eyes or move, but the dragon continued to stare me down.

"Oh, really? He speaks to you now?" My voice

sounded condescending, and I almost apologized for it. In response, the dragon blew out a puff of fire like he was blowing a kiss.

"Yes, he does, and he doesn't like you disturbing me right now, especially with your guest down-stairs." I backed out of her room and closed the doors behind me. I had forgotten entirely about Shay.

MY HAND RESTED on the small of Shay's back as I lead her down a series of hallways. This is what it was like on the bottom level of the compound. We had more than enough rooms down here, and I couldn't fathom why my father contorted the mansion again for Freya. Yes, I understood her importance to a certain extent, but showing favoritism usually did nothing but start wars. We didn't need any more of that around her, especially inside the coven. The robin's egg glue walls matched Shay's pantsuit, and she seemed happy enough walking the distance down the worn wood floors. Her heeled shoes clicked along as we walked.

"Wasn't this called something else back in the day?" Shay asked, hesitantly.

"What? The Compound?" I wasn't entirely sure

I was ready for the can of worms she was about to open. We had made it past many of the family quarters and were coming along the single witches housing. It was pretty much like a hotel or apartments, though you would never know just by looking at the outside. My father worked wonders in the courtroom and in architecture. The man had frightened me for many reasons growing up. Most of it had to do with the unknown.

"Yes," She smiled. Her canine teeth reminded me of a vampire's. I hadn't met many of them, but the look of them would haunt you to your core.

"Yes, it was called Coilette Maison." As the words left my lips, I knew I wasn't ready for the slew of questions that would come next. I didn't want to talk about Freya or her mother. I didn't want this new friendship to start off that way.

"Ah, how beautiful. I wonder why it changed." She quirked an eyebrow at me. As a witch, she had access to that knowledge.

"Feel free to ask my father, Jonathan, tomorrow when he meets with you." I unlocked her door with a small iron skeleton key and motioned for her to enter. She bowed her head forward, and her hair covered her face as she entered the beautifully furnished room. "You will be able to leave the room when he comes to fetch you tomorrow."

She looked up at me alarmed and tried to walk out of the door. She hissed as the wall lit up with electricity. "Why are you doing this?"

"It isn't my rule," I said, unease filling my voice. I would have rathered my father do this. "But I do agree with it."

She stepped away from the barrier that separated us. "Why?"

"It keeps the coven safe, especially when we don't know who we can trust." I briefly closed my eyes. "You won't be able to exit the room at all. You are practically living in an electric box. My father thought of everything when he started this a few weeks ago."

She nodded her head, accepting the terms of her being here. It could be much worse, though I also didn't know what my father had in mind. He liked truth spells too much, and they were painful. I had been at the end of his magic many times.

Shay closed the door before she glanced at me one last time. Her smile was full of pity, and I didn't like the taste it left in my mouth. I turned away from her room and didn't look back. It was getting late, and I needed to hear what my father had to say.

I COULDN'T HELP the anger that was bubbling to the surface. I had had to wait all night just to hear, what? Something I already knew and it had been kept from me my entire life!

"I was sent here when I was a baby, my mother was from the Mirror Realm. The Elven kingdom attacked, and she fled. We traveled many years before the Scandinavian coven took us in. My mother would jump back and forth between realms to see my father. Eventually, the High Priestess of the coven put a stop to it, but I saw where she hid her mirror." He looked away from me then and looked army mother sitting at his desk. "When my mother died, I still hadn't come into my magic. The Scandinavian people didn't know how to help me, so I traveled for much of my young adult life. I didn't go to school and didn't have the necessary paperwork to do much."

"How were you able to get into New Orleans then?" Ayre asked. She sat crossed legged on the floor in front of me. She carefully pulled at the tassels on the red and gold rug.

"Eventually my magic manifested, it was a long and painful experience. I later found out that my magic was having trouble because of the essence here in the Earth Realm. I should have died. My magic ended up warping because of that. That is why I don't have a magi." He shrugged and ran his hands down the front of his suit, all business. "I went back to my people and got my mother's things. I unwrapped the mirror, and after that, I searched for my father. My mother had kept a picture of him in one of her bags, and his clothing, in case he ever came for us."

Ayre frowned and looked back at the rug. Unshed tears shone in my mother's eyes, and I wondered what Freya was doing while we were stuck in here. I would have preferred to be anywhere, but here. I felt uncomfortable and confused.

"I was afraid you would die too, Sterling." His words startled me from my thoughts. "When the doctor laid you in my arms, I thought I was going to fall apart. I was terrified." For the first time in my entire life, the man I called Father had a soul. The stone-cold face he always wore was replaced with fear and regret. His lips that were usually pressed together in a harsh line were parted and vulnerable. "I found out too much about my lineage, and it frightened me. Many of the books in here are from there."

"What do you mean? Like you stole them?" I asked.

"Yes, I stole many things from the Mirror Realm, knowing very well that I would never return. I destroyed my mother's mirror when I found out that my father could have visited. I destroyed many of her things when I found out that he was the king."

Ayre spewed her water across the room. "What the actual hell?!"

"Cal and Armia are your siblings?" I shouted.

"No, my father was the true king before the mad king banished him. There is much to the story that I do not understand, nor do I care to." My father shoved his hands into his pockets and looked away from us. "I don't want the throne, and there has been a reason all of this has been a secret. Freya can't even know."

Ayre pushed herself from the floor and shook her head. "It isn't my secret to tell, but she will know one day. The High Priestess knows her people, and Vailen kinda knows everything already. Soooo, there is that."

Our father let out an exasperated sigh. "Indeed, but she has much to learn before that happens."

I actually agreed with my father on something. That was a first.

Our mother stood up and ran her fingers through her long hair before she spoke, "Go have some breakfast and try to act normal. I know this is a lot to take on, but we must remain calm and collected. If Sariah knows something is up, she will not hesitate in her plans."

Ayre was the first out of the study doors, she didn't look back and just kept shaking her heading, muttering about how crazy I was and intuitive. I wasn't precisely sure those two adjectives went together, but it was Ayre. Nothing about her seemed to make sense sometimes. I followed her out, wanting to get as far away from all of this as possible.

Shay was sitting at the bar in the kitchen, and Freya was biting into an apple. She wiped at the juice that was starting to spill down her bottom lip before she spoke, "Is Ayre all right? She seemed kind of shaken up." She frowned. "Well, now that I mention it, you are looking a little pale as well."

"No, everything is fine." I passed by her and opened the huge walk-in fridge. With as many people as we had around here, we had to be prepared for anything. Freya didn't say anything and took another bite out of her apple, while she narrowed her eyes at me.

Shay smiled at me brightly.

"I see you're in a better mood and you met Freya." Shay paused in the doorway at the tone of my voice. I wasn't very inviting, but I did have a lot to process. She looked back at the strawberry blond munching on her apple. Her face was expressionless.

"Yes, Jonathan cleared me this morning. I was kind of surprised by how early it was, especially for a truth serum." She leaned against the stainless-steel door. "Those things are nasty, and yes, Freya and I exchanged brief words."

"It's like he does it on purpose." I grabbed the carton of eggs and the gallon of milk. "I think he secretly likes to torture people."

Shay started to laugh until she saw my serious expression as I exited the fridge. "Oh, you're serious."

I shrugged my shoulders. "I don't know anymore, I can't keep up."

I watched Freya out the corner of my eye. Her top lip was pulled back slightly like she couldn't stand what she was witnessing. When I turned around fully, I realized what she was sneering at. Shay was sitting on the island, facing me and her skirt had ridden up her legs slightly. Her smooth dark skin was on display for anyone that came in the kitchen, but she didn't seem to mind. She gave me an inviting smile, and I couldn't help but turn away from the situation, which wasn't like me at all. I just couldn't handle the way Freya was staring me down.

"Do you think there's something in the fridge that Vailen could eat?" Freya said innocently.

"Who's Vailen?" Shay said, mild curiosity in her tone.

"You'll meet him soon enough." Freya tossed her apple core in the garbage and winked at me as she walked by. I wondered what she was playing at. I didn't like mind games, but I didn't think that was what she was doing either. If anything, I would have assumed that she was going after Shay. For what, I had no idea.

CHAPTER TWENTY-SIX

FREYA

"Y ou think you could do your sniffy voodoo thing on the new girl?" I asked Vailen as he paced in front of the window. I could feel his anxiety and knew he wanted to fly. I didn't know if it was our bond or not, but I wanted to feel the wind on my face too.

"Why? Do you feel like she's a threat to your safety or a threat to your possible romance with Sterling?" I didn't know if I was ever going to get over the fact that he was in my head.

I rolled my eyes dramatically. "Neither. I just think she's a hoe."

"I hate human slang. Can't we think of something more intelligent to call her?" Vailen stared at me with no humor in his eyes.

"Fine, I'll keep the human slang to myself."

"Please and thank you."

Ayre pushed the bedroom doors open then threw herself down on my bed. "I hate keeping secrets from you."

I frowned. "How do you tell someone to not disclose the information?"

Vailen watched us both before he shook his head and left the room. I was pretty sure most of the coven wasn't aware of his existence yet, and I didn't know how this was going to go over. I guess it had to happen sometimes and the sooner, the better.

"Do you think that's such a good idea?" Ayre watched him leave the room. Her hair was piled onto her head in a messy bun, and her dress was wrinkled. It was tied at the waist and dipped low in the front. From this view, all I could see was cleavage.

"I think it has to happen at some point. Plus, is anyone going to actually try to stop him from doing anything?" As I looked around my room, I decided that I needed more furniture soon. I hated not being able to leave. I wanted to live my life and go places. I loved New Orleans to a certain extent, I wanted to at least explore it with my new abilities.

"You do have a point there," she said. "Do you think this is too low cut?" She pulled at the neckline on her dress. I had to admit, she did look hot.

"What are we trying to accomplish here?" I asked, picking at my fingernails inconspicuously.

Ayre laughed and shook her head. "I might like someone."

"Why haven't I heard of this someone?"

"Well, we have been trying to get you back to New Orleans for a few weeks now and before that everything was happening all at once. I haven't seen much of him." She shrugged.

"Well, who is he?" I asked she had my full attention now.

"He's training to be one of the professors. He is in my father's office every evening. I promise that you will notice him soon enough. His name is Liam." She giggled like a little girl, and it made my heart happy. We deserved some happiness around here. Everything seemed to just suck.

Pretty soon our conversation was interrupted by the screams of terror. I couldn't keep the smile off of my face as I peeked through the bedroom doors. I could have laughed. Vailen had grown a good 40 feet and towered over the courtyard. I guessed that was an excellent way to make an entrance. A few of the witches were perched, ready to use magic to take him out while others looked at him curiously, probably realizing that he is the only dragon in existence and they shouldn't harm him. Vailen rolled his eyes and shrunk back down to his usual size. It seemed like he was just wanting to get a rise out of the coven and once he had succeeded, he was now bored.

"You aren't far from the truth, little witch." his voice purred in my mind, and I could just barely see him rolling his eyes as he walked away.

"At least he knows how to make an entrance," Ayre said leaning in the doorway.

"That's exactly what I was thinking. He seems like the dramatic type." I replied back.

"Are you sure he isn't supposed to be my familiar then?" she said as she giggled.

One minute I was there in front of Ayre, about to reply to her and the next I was in front of the coven. I had a strange burning sensation in my throat, and I almost fainted when I saw myself walk across the courtyard. But it also wasn't exactly me either, my eyes looked reptilian.

"Silly mortals, the bonding is completed. You cannot kill me, and you cannot kill my familiar." Vailen's voice came to life, spilling from my lips.

I could see Ayre practically throwing herself over the balcony in shock of what was happening. If I had been up there, like I was supposed to be, I would have been doing the same thing. I didn't think a familiar was supposed to be this powerful.

People gasped as lighting bounced on my fingertips, ready to play. I started to smell smoke, then realized it was coming from Vailen's snout. I still couldn't believe we had switched bodies. I didn't feel any different, besides the burning sensation in my throat and the agitation at Vailen. Vailen looked at me through my eyes and grinned. It was the weirdest experience I had to date. I had no doubt that there would be plenty more.

"Can I have my body back now?" I sent the thought to Vailen. I tried to sound as sweet as I possibly could, even though I was extremely agitated. When Shay and Sterling came running from the direction of Jonathan's office, I could feel the fire clawing its way up my esophagus. She was grasping his arm for support, looking between me and my body.

This couldn't get weirder.

"Sterling, tell these mortals to get used to seeing the big, bad dragon. This shouldn't be a spectacle."

Vailen tossed my head back and placed one of my hands on my hip.

Smoke was rising from my reptilian nostrils, and I was afraid if I sneezed, fire would explode from me. Sterling raised his hands toward me in surrender, and I just threw myself down on my scaled front legs. There was no use in trying to do anything. I would destroy the compound if I tried to even move an inch. I could feel the magic underneath my skin growing and retracting as if Vailen was still in control of this form as well. For some reason, I knew he did.

Just my luck.

A man broke through the terrified crowd and gave me a disgusted glare. I tried to keep the offense to a minimal, this was all Vailen's dramatic doing. "Why is she allowed back here? Didn't she run off to be with her mother, the traitor?"

The terrified witches around him soon became angry. They resembled a mob with all their crazed expressions and tense composer. This wouldn't be good.

Sterling's mouth formed a harsh line, and I wished I could have seen Ayre and how she was reacting all of this. "She is a victim, just like the rest of us."

"Really? How are we supposed to trust you? You have been seen entering and exiting her keep quite frequently." The man folded his arms over his chest, and the crowd nodded their heads. Sheeple. Didn't these people have a mind of their own?

Unlikely.

"I was there to come to an agreement with her on Freya's behalf. There is much to be discussed and thought out. Sariah is a powerful witch, and we have yet to find out what she wants with the city." Sterling looked above my head, and I had a feeling, he was looking to Ayre for some moral support. She was great at that. She seemed to be a beacon of hope to many as of late.

"Wouldn't you want the dragon on your side?" Vailen arched one of my eyebrows, challenging the young witch.

"No." The leader's feet were planted firmly, and his fists were squeezed tight.

"How stupid you are. You have the chance to be allied with one of the most powerful dragons of all time, and yet, you deny it. What a pity." Vailen held my hands out in front of me/him and lighting danced between them. It scared me and excited me that he knew this much about my power and my magi.

"That's enough, Vailen." Sterling took a step closer to us.

"Fine," Vailen purred.

I was shocked into my body almost as quickly as I had been taken out of it. My knees wobbled and failed me. I watched as the ground rushed up to my face, but I never hit the unforgiving cobblestones. Vailen's tale was wrapped around my waist, holding me steady. I touched his scales in reverence. They turned copper in the sunlight. He was truly magnificent.

"You are mine to protect, Shavile. I will never let harm befall you for as long as I shall live." His words made me look him in his eyes. "I will not take your body again unless you give me permission. I forget my power sometimes, please forgive me."

I nodded my head once, and he gently placed me back onto the ground. When I lifted my head and looked at Sterling, he gasped.

"What is it? What's the matter?" I touched my face subconsciously, expecting the worse.

"Your eyes." Oh, no, not again.

" What happened to them?" I turned an accusing glare onto Vailen. He let out a puff of irritated smoke and looked away, but just as he did, I noticed that his eyes were no longer green. They were purple.

Sterling pulled his cell phone out of his pocket and turned the screen around so I could see myself in the selfie camera. I swallowed. It couldn't be. My irises were slightly elongated to match Vailen's. They looked exotic and scary. Vailen's still looked the same, but the purple color made them look softer.

"We are officially bonded. No matter the distance, no matter circumstances, we are bound. I am yours to command." Vailen lifted his wings and pumped the air underneath them, almost in hazah. The wind from them hit me hard, and I had to squint my eyes. Everyone in the compound ducked and looked frightened.

Jonathan parted the crowd and looked around at all the faces. His eyes stopped on the leader of the revolt. "You know better, Jacobs." He glared at the growing crowd. "You are all dismissed. I had important council business to discuss. This better be important." Ayre had now come down the stairs and walked up to her father. She touched his arm tenderly, and I watched as his shoulders relaxed.

"We were not prepared for this." Jacobs sneered.

"Do you expect me to tell you everything that goes on around here? Are you a prince in line for the throne?" Jonathan sneered back. "No, I didn't think so. You are training to be a professor, and I will not tolerate this kind of behavior."

Professor? I wondered if he knew Liam.

"Yes, sir," Jacobs said, lowering his eyes to the ground. "I want to be a voice for our people one day. I want to sit on the council with you someday."

Jonathan's expression matched Sterling's. His lips were drawn tight. He looked up at my big dragon friend and his eyes narrowed. "So be it, but this is not the way to go about it. We are already having a civil war, we don't need any more foolishness. Witches have been disappearing. I am not sure it is by their own will or if Sariah is behind it." Jonathan pinched the bridge of his nose. "We must remain a united front."

Jacobs nodded his head, but his eyes were no longer on Jonathan. They were on Ayre. Something changed within them, but I couldn't put my finger on it. Ayre's eyes were on her brother. I imagined she was trying to soothe him in some type of way, but his body language was tense. Shay leaned against a pillar and watched Vailen with curious eyes.

I wanted to go over to her and see if she wanted to meet him, but I figured it was much too soon. I wasn't that good at being a friend anyway. Especially when I was confused about how I felt about Sterling. I didn't like how Shay was throwing herself at him, but it seemed like every woman did the same thing. Everyone except me and I wasn't about to change that. I didn't need anything complicated entering my life.

Ya know, it wasn't as if my long lost mother was the High Priestess of a witch coven from New Orleans and I had recently bonded with the last dragon in existence. No big deal.

I let out a sigh and turned toward Shay. She was now looking at me with a newfound curiosity. "Shay meet Vailen." I tried to keep my voice friendly, but I knew I was failing miserably at it.

"He's a big boy, isn't he?" What a dumb question.

I raised my eyebrows, trying not to say anything condescending. "Well, yes, he is a dragon."

"So I see." Her voice was clipped like she would rather be speaking to anyone but me, and I couldn't have agreed more.

"He's not that bad, I guess. I haven't known him for long, but he seems sweet."

She turned her nose up at me and marched away. Well, then.

"How are you feeling?" Sterling's concern made me jump out of my skin. I turned around to face him and felt my face flush.

CHAPTER TWENTY-SEVEN

STERLING

I didn't know what I had said to make her blush as hard as she was, but it was cute. It matched her hair almost.

"I'm not really sure how I am supposed to be feeling after all of that, but I guess all right." I tried to focus on Freya, but all I could hear was my father reprimanding Liam. I couldn't stand the man, and I hated the fact that my sister was infatuated with him.

She wasn't the only one that was for sure. Some of the students at the academy followed him around and always asked him questions. He was about the only competition I had when it came to the women in New Orleans. I could be honest with that. If they weren't after me, they were pining for him, and if I turned them down, they would go running to him. I couldn't imagine how it would go when he actually became a professor. My disdain for him grew by the minute and when he had tried to go after Freya and Vailen? I felt my power surge forward like it had never done before. I wasn't exactly the protective sort, but something snapped.

"I'm sure it took a lot of your energy and magic," I said, sympathetically. I couldn't stop looking into her eyes. They were fascinating but frightening.

"I have no idea what happened." Her face went grim. "I thought I was supposed to be the one in control. He is supposed to be my familiar. Ya know?"

"My father knows who he is. He is a powerful dragon. Queen Armia's father killed him. He was the last of his kind and the strongest." I shoved my hands into my pants pockets.

She nodded then wrinkled her eyebrows. "Who is this Shay character?"

"She said she is seeking refuge from something that happened in the Paris coven, though my father has yet to get any information on it from the council." I pulled at the buttons on my stiff Oxford shirt and thanked the essence. Without my magic, I would have never been able to survive the humidity of New Orleans. I sometimes hated the style I had acquired.

Freya looked away from me to Vailen and gazed at him curiously. "That Jacobs dude is a bit much."

I frowned, confused, wondering why she was calling Liam by his last name, but I went with it. "Yeah, he is passionate. I also think he's an entitled piece."

She turned back to me when she heard the animosity in my voice. "Do I sense jealousy?" She sounded amused. Her eyebrows were arched curiously as she licked her bottom lip.

She turned away from me, and I took the chance to admire her. She was wearing a big sweatshirt and cut off shorts. Her bare feet were a bright contrast against the cobblestones. Her back was ramrod straight, and her hair was tossed up carelessly in a bun.

Freya pulled a strand of hair away from her face and twisted it around her finger. I still couldn't figure out my fixation with her. Her petite body was cute, and the hourglass figure would give anyone with eyes fantasies, but it was her mind that had me. At least that was what I thought. It was the sassiness and the calculating look in her eye. It was like she had an old soul. Her eyes told me stories, stories that I yearned to hear, but I didn't know if I was ready for that kind of commitment.

It was one thing to sleep with a girl, but it was another to listen to her innermost thoughts. That was a territory that I had never been in. Though I was eager to explore it, I was also afraid. That kind of attachment came with a price.

To the hell with it. "Tell me what it was like growing up."

She whipped around, ready to defend her upbringing or prepared to defend herself. When she saw my curious expression, that I actually wanted to know her, she paused. I could see the uncertainty in her eyes. "It was tough."

"It's okay if you don't want to talk about it. It was out of nowhere, and you don't owe me a thing." I pushed my hands deep within my pockets.

"No one has ever genuinely wanted to know about me." She frowned.

"That's absurd, I am sure there is much to learn behind those pretty eyes." The compliment took me by surprise and by the look on her face, it did the same to her.

She opened her mouth to say something but was at a loss for words.

"I'm sorry, too soon." I ducked my head. For the first time in my life, I felt uncertain and insecure.

"No, it's just different. I'm not used to the good attention side of you." She shook her head slowly. "I've been waiting for the mean side to come out."

I pressed my lips together. I deserved that. I had been terrible. For whatever reason, I knew that this would happen. I knew that I would get stuck on her. I knew that I wouldn't be able to stop getting to know her once I started. I knew that once I had her, once I won her over, I would be the one that would be lost.

"And I'm going to make it up to you, every day for as long as I can until the memories of the past are made clean with good ones from the present." A smile tugged at my lips.

She narrowed her eyes at me, but her voice sounded relaxed. "We had to fight for everything that we wanted. We had to claw, scrape and kill for anything. You won't survive a day out there if you don't. I learned quickly. I watched the other children and knew their strengths and their weaknesses. Every single one of them took me for granted because they thought I was too small to amount for anything."

I didn't know what to say. We didn't watch the news. There was no need for us to dabble in human relations, that was what the council was for. We mainly just listened to a few things here or there to keep up appearances in the human world.

"If you were an older child, you didn't get adopted. At least, it was very rare. I did what I did to survive. Every day was different. It kept me on my toes." She shrugged and turned away from me again. She watched Vailen shrink to the size of a cat and lazily swat at a dragonfly. I chuckled at the site. Vailen must have known what I thought because he rolled his eyes and then rolled onto his back.

"I lived a very privileged life here. I know you probably don't think very highly of me for it." I gulped, now nervous.

"No," She shook her head, a few red strands of hair fell out of her bun and rested against her pale neck. "It is what it is, and if I went my entire life comparing things like that, I would be miserable. I just live and take it day by day. Plus, I get to live in all of this now." She spun around slowly. "I have more than what I deserve."

CHAPTER TWENTY-EIGHT

FREYA

Sterling's mouth dropped open. He was in shock. I knew he didn't believe what he was hearing, but it was the truth. I was more than grateful to have come upon my magi and my familiar. I didn't deserve any of it and yet, the universe or the essence, just kept giving me more.

He smiled and shook his head. I could just barely make out the words under his breath, "Perfect, just too perfect."

I didn't understand what he meant by that, and I wasn't about to ask. It already didn't make sense that he wanted to know more about me.

"Would you like to go to dinner or something?" His voice cracked on the last word, and he looked at me horrified.

I smiled. I had never seen him so flabber-gasted, it was adorable. He didn't seem to fall all over himself like this with other girls. I didn't mind it, it was a nice change. "Yes, I would like that."

Shay took that moment to appear in the court-yard and approach us. Well, Sterling.

I watched as Sterling's face changed and he put on a charming smile. I could feel my eyebrows furrowing. It was one thing to watch him be one way with other women, but it was another thing entirely to watch him transition to that person. Shay beamed as she got closer, too happy with the charm Sterling was throwing at her.

I rolled my eyes, and Vailen spoke in my mind."Your magic is winding up."

"What do you know about my magic?" I thought back.

"Much more than you do." He didn't sound egotistical in his response, but there was a hint of pride in his words.

"I can't even tell," I shook my head in frus-tration.

"Close your eyes," Vailen said, softly. "Take a deep breath. Focus on your energy."

I did as he instructed, but I couldn't feel any

energy. I shook my head again. Growing more frustrated.

"Focus on your anger. Make it real." when I didn't understand what he was talking about, he sent an image in my mind. It was a beautiful petite girl with red hot waves coming off of her. It took me a minute to realize that he had sent me an image of myself. I looked at him with surprise. He closed his eyes and spoke with in my mind again. "Imagine pulling that red back inside of yourself."

I closed my eyes and took a deep breath. I imagined the red energy floating into the sky, then I inhaled and imagined all the red going into my nose and mouth.

"That's it," Vailen whispered in my mind. I closed him off as I felt the whispers of magic tickling my face. "Simply incredible. Your magic works a little different than the other witches."

I opened my eyes and felt better than I had before. "What do you mean?"

"Every witch is different. They feel the essence and energy a little differently. Your mind is what's keeping your Magi from working with you." he said while he sat up and stretched.

I made my way to him and ran my fingers down the scales on his head. I sunk down to the hard ground and leaned against him. Sterling and Shay were leaning together, talking animatedly.

"What do you think about him?" I sent my thought to Vailen and looked around the courtyard. A few witches stood around, glaring at me. Ayre had disappeared and so had Jacobs, good riddance to him.

"He is confused about his feelings for you." Vailen's silky smooth voice coated my mind.

"That's not what I asked," I said, dejected.

"Then what are you worried with?" he replied. Anyone could see that he wasn't comfortable around me.

"I don't know, when we first met, he was so nasty to me," I said, trying my hardest to forget.

"I have to warn you," he said.

"About?" I watched Shay touch Sterling's arm affectionately. She leaned toward him and flipped her hair. I wondered if she practiced that.

"Through our bond, eventually, you'll get snippets of my memories, and I will get yours," he said, solemnly. "You won't get a warning either."

"What made you want to divulge that information now?" I asked, still focused on Shay and Sterling.

"I get little bits and pieces of your pain through

our connection." Vailen's tail thumped lazily behind us. "When my pain comes forward, it will, hopefully, be like nothing you have ever experienced."

His statement made me look down at my lap. I wondered what his pain was caused by and when and if I would actually feel it. I didn't get much from Vailen's side of the bond. I imagined it had a lot to do with how powerful he was. He didn't seem to need much practice.

"That's not true. This is very new to me. The last time I experienced a similar bond... it was with my mate." He closed his eyes, and I watched as smoke lifted from his nostrils. I laid my head on his broad back and didn't pry. I didn't know enough about dragons, and I didn't want to cause him unnecessary pain.

I CHECKED my hair for the fifth time. It looked the same, but I was beyond nervous. Sterling would be here any moment, and though I was physically ready, I definitely wasn't emotionally prepared. A knock on my bedroom door had me jumping through my skin. I smoothed down the invisible wrinkles on my dress and pulled the double doors open. My smile fell.

"Don't look so disappointed." Ayre pushed past one and threw herself on to my bed next to Vailen. "What are you up to anyway?" She paused and frowned. "You're wearing makeup."

"Yes," I didn't know if she would be happy or upset about the news I was going to drop on her. "Um, Sterling will be here any moment."

She rolled over and frowned at me. "What do you want from him? Is he going to take you on a double date with him and Shay?" She chuckled at herself. Vailen rolled his eyes.

"We actually have a date," I whispered, unsure of myself.

She made a face and sat up. "But he's been obsessed with Shay lately..." she trailed off.

I shrugged my shoulders. I tried not to look into it too much. He had followed through with his request and had approached me a few days after everything had gone down with Jacobs and the rest of the witches.

Other than that day, everything had been quiet. Vailen continued to teach me and coach me with my powers. My magi was more than willing to do the work, as long as my brain stopped getting in the way.

I had been in the courtyard, trying my hardest to get into meditation, when Sterling startled the hell out of me. He just quietly sat down in front of me, and when I opened my eyes, I had let out a shriek of terror.

Other witches had whipped around in surprise, and Vailen retreated back to my quarters. Lately, he had been fed up with the extra attention and fled if too many people came around him at once.

Sterling and I had spoken a few words, and he told me he was ready to pull out the date card. I had been wondering when he would come to his senses.

But now as I waited for him to meet me, I wondered if I had made a mistake. Ayre was playing a game on her phone and not paying me any attention anymore.

When Sterling knocked on the door, it startled me out of my thoughts. For once he wasn't wearing a suit, and I immediately felt self-conscious of my dress. His eyes beamed as he took me in and Ayn made a funny noise before she slid past us and disappeared into the courtyard.

"You look beautiful," Sterling said, softly

"Thank you." I gazed over my shoulder at Vailen still asleep on my bed. "Don't wait up!" He didn't even open his eyes. He probably slept more than a house cat.

Vailen's voice popped into my head. "I eat cats for breakfast."

"You're just plain gross." I threw over my shoulder as I followed sterling out into the humid Louisiana night.

Sterling stopped and gave me a puzzled look. "Who?"

"Oops, sorry, Vailen. We hate a weird telepathy thing." I shrugged, and he continued walking again. I tried to stay focused, but the way his dark wash jeans hugged his thighs was making me a bit scatterbrained.

"I wondered about that. I've seen yall sit in the courtyard together. You'll make faces at him, but you don't speak." He stopped and let me catch up with him. I had fallen behind watching his behind. I was mortified.

Sterling walked us to a small Cajun restaurant in the Quarter and jazz swam around us in the thick air. The conversations were, and the smiles were light. When we were finished with dinner, he extended his hand to me and nodded to the dimly lit area. I placed my hand in his much darker and rougher palm. He pulled me to the middle of the room and into his arms like a pro.

Our movements were fluid and comfortable. There was no tension in our bodies. His fingertips brushed my hair away from my face, and he leaned in close. "This is not a scene that I frequent, but I could get used to it."

I nodded my head, in complete agreement. But then something happened that I should have anticipated. A blond woman stared us down from the doorway. She marched in our direction, and I hoped that she would just continue on, That it wasn't as she was after.

No such luck. She poked Sterling's shouldn. When he pulled away from me, his face was in complete shock.

"This must be why you can't return my calls." Her voice sounded familiar, but I couldn't place it. It was high pitched with a slow drawl. She scrunched up her face as she looked at me. "You!"

I took a step back, not wanting to be apart of whatever was unfolding.

The woman continued to advance in my direction. "You're the one that was in Sterling's bedroom that night." It clicked. She was the woman that

Sterling had been preoccupied with the night Ayre brought me to the compound. The night Sterling found me in the bed he was about to put to use. The night his hatred started. "He's not that good in bed. I hope you haven't already experienced how lousy he is."

Sterling finally got his mouth to work. "Must not hate been that bad you tried for seconds."

At that, I was done. I wasn't naive, but I also wouldn't be put in these embarrassing situations. So much for being a new place to frequent. Everyone was staring at us now, and even the band had stopped to see about the commotion. The woman continued to scream in Sterling's face, that he didn't even notice me slip from the restaurant. As I went, I saw the sympathetic looks thrown my way. It left an awful taste in my mouth.

I could hear Sterling shouting my name, but I continued on. I pushed through crowds of people until I could barely make out the alley that leads to the compound. I looked both ways before I crossed the street and as I was stepping onto the curb, I slipped. The hard concrete bit into my hands and knees. I whimpered in pain and pushed myself back up. I looked up to the night sky and rubbed my hands down the front of my dress, trying to get the pebbles to free themselves from my skin.

I barely registered the pain at the back of my skull as something hit me. I could hear Sterling shouting my name again, just as everything went black.

EPILOGUE

All I could hear was screaming and pain. The fear was thick in the air, and I knew I wasn't in New Orleans anymore. Nothing about my surroundings was recognizable except maybe the terrain. The soft pink grass called to me, but I wasn't in control here. My head whipped to the left, and guttural words tore from my throat, but it wasn't my voice that I heard. "Callia! Callia!" Panic swelled within my chest and the body I was inhabiting took a sharp dive in the air. I hadn't realized I was flying until that moment.

"Callia! Drake!" The words burned up my throat, and tears pooled in my eyes. Why was I talking if it hurt so damn bad? Then I noticed the smoke and devastation on the ground, the people running for dear life and the monsters that had been slaughtered. Not monsters, dragons.

No.

I knew exactly where I was.

I was in Vailen's mind, and I was reliving his most painful memory, but what had made it surge forward like this?

Vailen drove the ground and let out a scream of pain. There in front of us was an iridescent white dragon, every- thing about her was fierce and feminine. She blinked open her eyes, and I felt so much love course through the dragon. It made my heart ache because I knew what was to happen next. I tried to turn away, to close my eyes, but I knew what happened next. Her crystal blue eyes pleaded with us to leave and pretty soon I could hear her words in Vailen's mind.

"Please, find our son." Her voice was silky and smooth.

"I can't leave you, Callia." Vailen nudged her with his nose, urging her to get up.

"I can't fly with you. I am too badly injured. If our unborn is to live, you must let me rest here. The Tyrant King won't come back." Callia spoke softly. It wasn't the Tyrant King that worried Vailen, but he did as she requested even though it tore him apart to leave his true mate.

Vailen closed his eyes and pushed up from the grass. The air caught perfectly under his wings, and he was up soaring in mere seconds. HIs head went left then right, frantically searching the ground for his son. I didn't know how he could see through any of the smoke or fires. It seemed like all that was left was death.

That was when two figures below caught Vailen's eye. A man in black armor was facing off with a red dragon, a dragon that looked too much like Vailen. I knew it had to be Drake. Vailen circled from above watching his son go blow to blow with the Tyrant King. I could just barely hear Vailen's painful thoughts. Everything in his mind was chaos.

Something distracted Drake behind his opponent, and he paused. It was enough time for the king to move in and deliver a fatal blow. Vailen dove from the sky screaming and blowing fire everywhere, but it did nothing. Something was holding Drake captivated and he wouldn't move. Vailen fell to his son's body and shielded him from the king's final strike. Pain pierced through Vailen's side, but he didn't feel it. His grief had overwhelmed him to sacrifice his life for his child. His sacrifice was for nothing. As he faded from the world, he watched his only son die. Right before he was gone, he heard his mate let out her final cry too.

All was lost.

Vailen hadn't been lying when he said the pain I would feel would be the worst pain I had ever experienced. It was gut-wrenching and like a knife in your soul. I gasped for breath, trying to get my bearings together until I realized there was no need to gasp or breathe. All I could tell was that cold water was covering my body and everything was cold. I didn't know what was up or what was down. There was nothing. I was stuck in the void of not being alive or dead.

All was lost.

LOOKING FORWARD TO BOOK 2?

WELL, LUCKY YOU! YOU GET AN EARLY
EXCLUSIVE TO BOOK 2, FIXATED.
COMING SOON!

Pain

It was all I felt. It left a gapping hole inside my chest.

I knew the moment Freya was taken, but with her unconscious, there was no way I was going to be able to track her. I flew around the giant empire that Sariah had created and perched on one of the beams sticking out from the side of it. Vines had wrapped around the metal and exposed beams and almost made the monstrosity look pretty. I closed my eyes and tried to calm my heart and my breathing. The memory had come out of nowhere, and the pain had been renewed.

I had lost her. I had underestimated the witches. I had underestimated Sterling. He was just as devastated as anyone, but he was to blame, unfortunately. He let her get away. A woman alone in the Quarter was enough to raise alarm, but a powerful witch that was wanted? He should have never let her out of his sight. I should have known it was a terrible idea for her to go on a date. Now I was stuck here beating myself up. I shrunk myself down a few more inches and crawled to the wall.

I could hear Sariah screaming. "What do you mean you can't bring me the steel that killed the dragons?"

Queen Armia sighed. "We had it destroyed when my father died."

"There is no one in your kingdom that could recreate it?" I could hear Sariah pacing back and forth.

"No, my father killed the weapons master before they marched to battle. He was too afraid he would create something else even more powerful than himself." Armia sounded annoyed.

"You must figure this out. Their bonding is complete. The only way to keep any damage from happening is to keep them separate." Sariah said matter of fact.

Red hot rage was all I could taste as I grew to the most significant size imaginable. I towered over her little kingdom and lit it up. I no longer cared for the beings that lived within it, I no longer cared for anything. All I felt was anger and fire. I heard screams and explosions, and I had no doubt that they were going to try to fight me off, but I continued to pour my white fire down on them like the fiery wrath of God. I watched as Sariah ran for her life and I chased after her, I wanted her out of my new city. I wanted her gone for good. There was nothing that I could do to help Freya, but I would take care of the nuisance problem.

There was a part of me that told me to follow her, that she would lead me to Freya, but I knew the time would come. There was also a tiny bit of fear that Freya was left in the building I had melted to the streets.

ACKNOWLEDGMENTS

Goodness, there are always so many people to thank and I feel like I fall short each time. So here goes nothing!

I have to thank my dear friend, Tori, that loved my first series and loves this one even more. She would start reading as soon as I finished a section and if thats not dedication, I don't know what is. Thank you for letting me bounce ideas off of you and for encouraging me. I doubt this would have been possible without your faith in my creativity.

I would like to thank my husband for encouraging me to live my dreams and to constantly go after them, even if they are expensive. You always make sure I have the best and I don't know how I deserve you.

My family is next because without my mom and stepdad, I know I wouldn't get hardly anything done. They take my rowdy toddler when I need them to for author events or just so I can clear my head. I would be lost without you both.

My graphic designer, Jay, who always goes above and beyond for me. I KNOW I would be lost without you and I probably would refuse to publish haha. Your covers have propelled my confidence and continue to inspire me everyday. I simply want to write so I'll be able to get you to do a cover for me.

My little Mason, even though he can't read now, someday I hope he has a love for it as much as I do. Mason, you inspire adventures and hilarity in my stories. You give me life through my sometimes dark days. You constantly keep me on my toes. You're almost four years old, Happy Early Birthday baby.

ABOUT THE AUTHOR

A. Lonergan comes from a small town in southern Louisiana. She loves to cook, chill out with her family and her dogs (One is secretly a wolf. No really he is.), and get creative with all things makeup. She loves to meet new people, so feel free to connect!